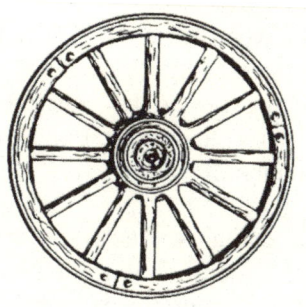

SOOKIE'S SILENCE

*Westward Home and
Hearts Mail-Order Brides #16*

Marisa Masterson

SOOKIE'S SILENCE

This book is a work of fiction. The names, characters, places, and incidents are all products of the author's imagination and are not to be construed as real. Any resemblances to persons, organizations, events, or locales are entirely coincidental.

Sookie's Silence ©2021 Marisa Masterson
Cover Design by Virginia McKevitt
        http://www.virginiamckevitt.com
Editing by Amy Petrowich
Formatting by Christine Sterling

1st Ed.

TABLE OF CONTENTS

ACKNOWLEDGEMENTS

A huge thank you goes to my husband, Trevor, and our friend Bob. Both had to listen to details about Sookie as this book traveled from my mind to the page. Bob taught deaf students and answered questions about sign language. He kindly listened to my explanation for each sign I created and added his ideas.

AUTHOR'S NOTE

In this book, you will see bible written without a capital B. While I know this choice bothers some, please understand that this is the correct way to write it. Nevertheless, I wanted to share with you that I think of it as capitalized since it seems to be a title. If I wrote it as the *Holy Bible*, it would be capitalized.

One more thing. I created a language for my mute heroine. Please take a look at the glossary if you become confused by those signs while reading.

CHAPTER 1

Bailey's Meadow, Nebraska
Early April 1871

The baby sobbed in her bed. Onie Hastings left the stove and hurried into the small bedroom where Letty cried pitifully. The sobs tore at him. He was sure she never cried like this at his sister's house.

The little one caught sight of him and leaned away when he reached for her. Those heart-wrenching cries turned into angry wails. As he lifted her, she pushed against his chest.

"Maaamaaa! Mama! Mama!" Her sweet voice bristled with anger and wanting as she said that name.

He tried to comfort her as best he could. Patting her back awkwardly, he crooned to her. "You're fine. I know you want Auntie, but you're here with Daddy."

The crying rose in volume. Onie wanted to cover his ears. Instead, he carried Letty to the kitchen. As he entered that room, acrid smoke filled his nostrils.

Dinner!

Another meal ruined. He knew that even before he awkwardly balanced Letty to pull the pot of soup from the stove. He burned his palm and fingers on the hot handle and upset the baby again. She sent up a howl of anger. When Onie plugged his mouth with the burned fingers, she stuck a thumb into her own, creating instant quiet.

Taking the hurt fingers from his mouth, Onie reached into a cupboard for his butter dish. Not bothering with a knife, he used the burnt hand to awkwardly lift the lid and run the injured fingers over the pale-yellow ball. He was desperate to coat the burns which already blistered. Really, he was the only person other than Letty who ate the butter. What did it matter if he stuck his fingers into it?

Plopping Letty into a kitchen chair, he tied a flour-sack towel about her middle and knotted it behind the chair. That done, he sat across from her and stared at the little girl. She resembled him but was a stranger, and he needed to change that.

"Letty, my girl, we're in for a world of changes. Auntie Ruby had her baby today. She can't be takin' care of you day and night now. Not like before."

At the mention of Ruby, Letty started to mewl as she mouthed, "Mama. Mama."

Her response was no surprise to Onie. He sent the baby to his sister when the little one was only a few months old. Now, almost a year later, Letty's bond to Ruby would not be easily broken.

Not that he wanted that. Only, he was free now of the false charge that chased him west. He had a home in Bailey's Meadow. His freighting business prospered, and the town even chose him as its sheriff. The last item he needed to fix was his family.

He knew he lacked any abilities resembling housewifery. Onie trained as a teacher not a housekeeper. He always expected Alicia to take care of the home. Her death soon after Letty's birth rocked his secure world. Her father's charge of theft against him stole any remaining security. It was why he gave the baby to his sister.

How to make a home for Letty now that Ruby wanted him to reclaim the baby? The conversation from a few days prior echoed in his mind.

"It's now or never, Onie. She stays with me as my daughter unless you take her home when I have this baby."

Ruby had patted her very round stomach lovingly. A former spinster, Ruby married a man well into his thirties. The two of them were overjoyed to be able to have a baby together, he knew, even though they already had a child from Elias's first marriage.

Ruby claimed Frank as her own, true. Nonetheless, she glowed whenever she spoke of the new member of their family. She once mentioned that she had been sure her age would prevent them having a baby together. For his part, Elias smiled a silly grin when he looked at his wife. Their baby seemed to be only a bonus for this man. A bonus that made that grin downright loony.

Earlier today, little Frank ran to the combination freight warehouse and jail and announced about the birthing. Immediately securing the building, Onie took off for Ruby's home. He gathered the bag Ruby packed with Letty's clothes and snagged a few of her toys.

All the while, Ruby let out occasional low groans in a bedroom across the hall. Those sent him hurrying Letty's belongings to his small home. Finally, he returned for his daughter and took her away from the only home she knew.

Now they stared at each other. Letty pouted and her father frowned. A thought that poked and prodded him over the last few days filled his mind. He voiced it aloud to his daughter.

"I need a wife and you need a mother." Tired resignation colored his voice as he admitted the truth.

Suddenly, another memory teased his mind. Donald Bailey the town's mayor and founder had approached Onie the week before about teaching. "We need a school to make this a true town. You're a teacher so why not start one for us?"

Onie refused politely. With his business and now the law in town, he had no time. Especially since he had Letty to watch over. But if a wife came who was also a trained teacher?

He ran both hands through his honey-colored hair and sighed. Honest with himself, he had to admit he needed a woman. His morals did not allow for intimacy outside the marriage bed. He could have someone to take care of his daughter and home.

During the day, the woman would teach the town's children. Then they would cuddle in his bed at night. She could make his life a whole lot sweeter.

Letty let loose pitiful cries. Baffled, he stared at her as she pounded on the table. "M—m..."

"Bet you want milk."

The cries stopped as the little girl said, "Yeah." She could not manage the *s* sound yet so her *yes* came out as the slang word.

"Good enough. Daddy'll get you a cup of it."

Onie raised the lid and pulled up the cold box from under his kitchen floor. Quickly grabbing the jar filled with milk from the one cow Elias kept at the livery, he poured some into a tin cup.

Smiling he placed the cup into the eleven-month-old's outstretched hands. She awkwardly tried to hold it to her mouth. In an instant she dumped the contents down her front. That started the horrid wails once again.

He groaned. Then he untied the damp towel and lifted the soggy baby. Her dress was wet. As he carried her to the bedroom, Onie realized her bottom was soaked also.

"How'd that milk get down to your bottom, Letty sweet?"

Realization had him wanting to slap a palm to his forehead. He would have if his hands had been empty. Of course, she would need a diaper change. He hoped Ruby packed diapers in her things.

"Letty, we really need a mama for you."

He would write the same matchmaker who joined Ruby and Elias. She did a good job for them. And he was much easier to live with than Elias. At least, Onie thought so.

She could find him a wife in jig time and his problems would be solved. Why, he would even send the money for a train ticket with his letter.

Later that evening, Letty's screams, then cries, then whimpers faded in that order as she grew tired and fell asleep. Finally, he could focus on a letter to the matchmaker. For the first time that day, Onie felt a niggle of happiness about his family's future.

Sitting at the kitchen table, he stared down at the sheet of paper. Dipping the steel pen into a bottle of dark liquid, he let its tip flow across the page as he penned the letter with his flowing, practiced script. Onie wanted to impress on both Mildred Crenshaw, the matchmaker, as well as any prospective bride that he was an educated man.

Dear Mrs. Crenshaw,

The match you made for my sister, the former Ruby Hastings, and Ezra King, actually Elias Kline, greatly impressed me. So much so, that I want to entrust my family's future to you.

I am, sadly, a widower. My young daughter badly needs the care of a mother. For myself, the touch which a woman brings to a man's home would be very appreciated.

Any woman you send west to marry me would be well cared for. This I can easily assure you. I am both a successful businessman who runs a freighting company as well the sheriff in Bailey Meadow, Nebraska. Townspeople say that they trust and admire me.

As for a potential bride, I do have some requirements. She must be no more than twenty-six years in age. I would like a blonde woman so that any children we have will be blonde like myself. Also, I do fancy petite women.

My last requirement may pose the greatest difficulty. The bride must be an experienced teacher. The town has asked me, a former teacher, to start a school. I have no time for that and would ask you to find a woman who can bring education to this growing town's children.

Perhaps I ask too much of you. As I read over this letter, I know that I am steadfast about two of the requirements in the woman you choose. Her age and education must meet what I specified in this missive.

As I wrote at the start of this letter, I trust you. There is no need for the bride to correspond with me. I am so confident that you will select the right woman to join my small family that I am enclosing funds for her travel as well as for your fee.

Please, we eagerly await the woman who will complete and care for my family while she also brings education to waiting children. Is this too much to ask? I fear so, and yet I have great hope that you will find this paragon.

Sincerely yours,

Onyx Hastings

Before sealing the letter, he pulled the book of checks from the small secretary in his pocket-sized parlor. Carefully, he penned an amount he considered sufficient. Blotting it, he waved the check to dry the ink and smiled. In only two or three weeks, he could have a bride and mother here. All problems would be neatly solved.

The next day, he delivered the letter to Plattsmouth since he needed to collect a shipment from that much larger town's depot. Sending it from a large town guaranteed that he would get a wife faster. At least in his mind it did.

There would be no need in the future to beg his sister's mother-in-law for help with Letty. He hated asking for help from anyone. The woman joyfully took the baby every time. She never made him feel badly about asking. It was only his stubborn pride.

Weeks passed without a response. When he did hear from Mildred Crenshaw, it was in person. She arrived three weeks to the day after he mailed the letter.

"I wanted to meet Ruby's baby." The small, plump woman sat on Ruby's dark blue sofa and cuddled little Joy Lynn to her bosom.

The smile she wore as she looked at the tiny infant faded when she met Onie's gaze. "Too, I feel I should interview you. Finding a teacher-bride to fit your personality may be tricky."

"Why should that be so? I am able to provide well, don't drink, and have never hit a woman." He made no effort to temper his disgruntled tone.

The older woman gave a clipped nod of her chin and stared solemnly. *As if she's peering into my soul.*

For a brief moment, the look pierced the blanket of pride he wrapped tightly around himself. Would she be satisfied with what she glimpsed inside him? Then he inwardly laughed at his fanciful thought.

No matter what, Onie determined to impress this woman during her visit.

CHAPTER 2

Arnolds Corners, Massachusetts
April 1871

Wearily, Sookie Donaldson climbed rickety steps leading to the apartment she shared with Renee, her sister. Really, Wren rather than Renee since the family had called her this since she was a very little girl. Both she and Sookie continued to use their nicknames even though neither were children.

The night had been long. One of the businesses employing her to clean asked her to lime the outhouse. That really was a man's job. Desperate though to hang onto the client, she did it. Afterward, the disgusting smell clung to her body and clothes. It filled her nostrils and continued to remind her of the hideous experience.

Each step higher to the small, dismal apartment brought up the horror of the last five months. The climb was so different than ascending the wide stairs to her comfortable room at the home her parents owned. The polished oak banister there aided her climb. Here, the steps often shifted under her feet as she made her way upward without a handrail.

That solid brick home disappeared as if an illusion. Vanished in the same way her secure future after the accident. The same way her voice had.

Countless times, she wished her mother had not suggested visiting a sick friend. A friend they never reached. The accident changed everything.

Stopping outside the scarred door, Sookie reached her fingers under the high collar of the dark shirtwaist. She fingered the ragged scar at the base of her throat. It seemed to come alive, flushing warmly at her touch. The spot continued to heal nicely, or so the doctor told her. Warmness there was nothing to worry about.

Removing the hand, she took a key from her pocket and jammed it into the antiquated lock. Sookie tried not to consider whether that lock and the skeleton key really protected them. Could someone break into their home, such as it was?

The neighborhood teemed with any number of thugs who threatened their safety. Still, it was the best she could afford for Wren. The safest she could find when a trusted person drove them from their real home.

As Sookie opened the door, her sister's face peeked around it. The older sister squeaked her surprise. The girl should be gone at nine in the morning.

Why was Wren home and not at school? Sookie quickly rubbed her stomach and then lightly thumped her head to ask about her health.

"No, my stomach is fine and I don't have a headache." Wren's voice bubbled with a restrained giggle.

Then the girl's gleeful mouth turned downward. "What happened to you? Ugh! You have to change quickly."

Before Sookie mimed a question or an explanation for her sister, a voice surprised her from their small parlor. "Nonsense, Renee. I am family. Bring Susan Kay in here to see me."

Sookie's eyebrows rose and her lips rounded to silently mouth, "Who?"

"No dallying. Come in and greet me, Susan Kay."

The mention of her real name created dread in Sookie's middle. She only heard that name before one of her parents punished her. Would this visitor bring them more trouble?

The elegantly dressed woman who rose from the room's single chair stepped around the ripped sofa and held out an inviting hand, palm up. Her clothing and manners brought a longing to Sookie. The woman somehow reminded her of the mother she lost only months before.

The stranger's clothing fit the elegant air of the woman. A mauve jacket trimmed with gray covered a walking dress of the same color and material. She had a lovely piece of blue jewelry pinned to the lapel. A Patek Phillippe keyless watch if Sookie was any judge of it.

Along with the gray buttons of the jacket, it was a very attractive outfit. Sookie shrank back from the woman because of it. Her own filthy clothes compared to this beautiful ensemble stirred up feelings of loss and had her choking back tears. Not tears for the clothes she no longer had but for the parents who had provided them.

When she would have bolted towards the apartment's single bedroom, the woman grabbed onto her hand. "No, don't bother chang—"

She broke off, quickly dropping Sookie's hand and reaching into a hidden pocket. She pulled out a delicate linen hanky and covered her nose. A familiar scent of lavender rose from the linen, somehow seeping past the stench in Sookie's nostrils. Her mother had used that scent in all of her dresser sachets.

"Oh my! What have you gotten into, you poor dear?"

Sookie shrugged slightly and focused on the woman's face rather than answering. Not that she could easily answer a stranger. Her gestures and mimes worked with Wren, but others would scarcely recognize them.

The prettily garbed woman looked very familiar. Her weary mind struggled and finally drew a name from her past. Mildred Crenshaw, her mother's cousin. While her mother often mentioned the woman when telling tales from her childhood, Sookie could count on one hand the number of times she and this woman actually met.

Stunned to see her in their dingy apartment, Sookie turned to Wren and rapidly signed *why*. While she recovered that first month after the accident, she and Wren worked out signs. First, they wrote a word and then created a gesture to go with it. Repeatedly using them, this became a secret language between the sisters.

The younger sister answered without translating for the cousin. "To check on us. She grew concerned when I wrote to her and explained the loss of our home and Father's share of the business."

Wren glanced uncertainly between the woman who once again sat on the chair and her sister. "Remember? I told you I wrote her."

With a bob of her chin, Sookie sighed. She retreated to the bedroom. There she contented herself with the pitcher of cool water and a cake of soap rather than a soak in the tin tub. Her hair would have to wait even though odors wafted from it. At least the rest of her now gleamed rosy pink from the scrubbing she gave her body and her clothes were clean.

Wearing the simple black shirtwaist and black skirt which comprised her best outfit, she checked the mirror once more. No dark brown curls escaped the simple style at the back of her head. Twisting those curls into a bun proved difficult, making Sookie long for the fashionable hairstyles of her youth. At twenty-five and after four years as a spinster teacher, she knew only a no-nonsense bun would be appropriate.

The brown eyes and pale face that stared back at her from the mirror wore a defeated frown. Any thought of her years as a teacher did that. She enjoyed her job and put her whole body and soul into it. That the schoolboard could so easily dismiss her after the accident hurt like a betrayal from a friend.

For what had to be the hundredth time she mentally chastised, "No one is irreplacable."

23

Sookie pinned her mother's locket brooch to the high collar, their only piece of jewelry after the sisters sold what they quickly gathered before being forced out of the house. She took a last look at the dark-haired, tired woman in the mirror and sighed.

Forget me not flowers created by pearls and diamonds decorated the gold and blue enameled piece at her throat. While they could realize a great deal of money from it because of the gold and jewels, Sookie refused to think of parting with it.

Her mother always insisted the brooch held a great secret. If something was hidden inside, Sookie had yet to discover it since the clasp had jammed. She feared breaking it too much to force it.

Heading to the parlor started her trembling. The woman she was scarcely resembled anyone Mildred Crenshaw would remember. Still, she needed to get out there and introduce the new version of Susan Kay Donaldson to her relation.

Leaving the room, she caught the last few words of Mildred Crenshaw's conversation with Wren. "This will not do. Not at all."

At the open doorway to the pocket-sized parlor, Sookie stopped and flapped her right hand out with the palm up. Wren saw the sign and immediately explained. Her sister was like that, a person who easily reassured others.

"Cousin Milly has an idea you need to hear. A way for you to return to the schoolhouse."

Not wanting to be rude, the older sister did her best to discreetly point at the woman followed by the sign for *speak*. Milly, as Wren called her, watched her closely. Her pinched lips and moist eyes let both sisters know how deeply the woman felt about their situation. At least, she thought that must be why their visitor's lips drooped.

"Please, Cousin Milly, tell Sookie about settling the west and sending brides."

At the word bride, the mute woman raised her brows and rounded her eyes. The last five months taught her to over dramatize reactions to compensate for her inability to vary the tone of her signs. She gestured *what* to her sister, letting her alarmed expression carry her concern.

Wren's tone soothed as she moved to the doorway and took her older sister's arm. Patting it, she led the other woman to the sofa. There, they both sat, ready to listen to their mother's cousin.

The elegant woman who sat in their shabby chair was small and pleasantly plump with light brown hair attractively pinned under a flower-trimmed hat. Sookie's mother had been tall and slender with almost-black, curly hair that she gifted to her older daughter. Even so, Milly Crenshaw's sudden smile brought a lump to the younger woman's throat. Her mouth and its movement echoed their mother's expression almost exactly.

That smile melted Sookie's resistance. She nodded at the woman and hesitantly returned the expression. Of course, this cousin would not understand that the hesitation was meant to send a message. Wren would explain that, if she thought it was important.

Over the past months since the accident, the younger sister grew protective of her older sibling. Quite a switch from their prior relationship, when Sookie mothered and protected the girl who was seven years her junior. Wren's protective instinct appeared as she interpreted her sister's expression.

"My sister often speaks through facial cues, ma'am. At the moment she is ready to listen, though she can't understand how being a bride and teaching school go together." Wren glanced at her sister to be

26

sure she stated the concern correctly and Sookie nodded.

Milly's attractive face creased as her smile broadened. It was nearly wrinkle-free even though Sookie knew the woman was around her own mother's age of fifty. "My but I have a surprise for you then because I do know a way to bring the two together."

She paused meaningfully. "That is, if you are willing to entertain the idea of marrying a responsible, kind man living in the West."

Sookie's lips compressed as she considered that. She widened her eyes as she nodded. Then she rubbed her right hand down her left forearm. Turning to Wren, she waited for the girl to explain.

"Sookie believes that would be best for us if she did marry."

Raising a hand, the older sister opened her soundless mouth. Next, she tapped her scarred throat and covered her eyes. Milly looked from the older to the younger sister for an explanation. Wren covered Sookie's hand in a comforting movement before speaking.

"My sister is worried that the man will refuse a woman who can't speak." A mute nod by Sookie accompanied this interpretation.

With a wave of her small, plump hand, the cousin dismissed that. "Actually, this man taught deaf children here in Massachusetts before heading to Nebraska."

Accurately interpreting the shaking of Sookie's head, the older woman soothingly continued with her hands making downward motions in front of her chest. "I know that's not exactly the same as being mute, but it is close enough for him to understand your disability."

On the sofa, the perspective bride shifted and then nodded with a small shrug. Milly rushed on to explain further. "I've matched several couples and actually traveled to Nebraska to meet Onyx Hastings, or Onie as he's called by friends and family."

A faraway look came over Milly Crenshaw, something Sookie wondered at. Seeing the other woman crook her eyebrow, the matchmaker explained.

"I matched his sister Ruby with her husband. I was just remembering the handsome baby girl the woman birthed recently. While visiting to interview Onie, I enjoyed several cuddles with her sweet little Joy."

As Milly watched, Sookie hugged arms around herself. After that, she folded her arms to move them as if rocking a baby. Possessing a quick mind, the older woman correctly interpreted the gestures without Wren's help.

"I love babies, too. Perhaps more so because I was never blessed with any of my own."

A sad sigh slipped past tightly compressed lips before the cousin became business-like. "But back to the marriage. Onie is a widower with a small child. He needs a wife willing to also teach school three days per week."

Holding up five fingers, she wiggled the littlest finger. Milly smiled and slightly raised her shoulders. "I don't know why three and not five days as usual. You will need to ask him that."

"You're doing very well understanding my sister, Cousin Milly," Wren chirped happily from her place on the sofa.

"She's very expressive. I believe her students will catch on quickly to her language."

Nodding at Wren, Milly smiled at Sookie. "Having Renee with you to teach the gestures early on will speed their learning so they can understand you."

Tapping her chin, Milly's smiling face turned serious. "What do you think, Susan Kay?"

Wren answered, not waiting for Sookie to sign her displeasure. "Please, Milly, call us Wren and Sookie. The other names are used only for signing documents and such."

With a clipped bob of her head in response, the older woman repeated her question. "What do you think, Sookie?"

The sisters exchanged looks. The woman in question flapped her right hand out with the palm up. Then she tapped her temple and pointed at Wren. Their cousin, being a bright woman, understood that the older sister wanted Wren's opinion on this move.

Wren lifted her sister's hand, squeezing it tenderly. "If you are willing to marry, I think this is the answer to our nightly prayer. We've asked the Lord for a safe home and a way for you to teach. Both are waiting for us."

Sookie nodded, and this time flapped her right hand with the palm down. Wren looked from her sister to their cousin to explain. "She wants to know when we would go."

At the question, Milly chuckled. "That town wanted you there yesterday. Yes, they are very eager for a teacher since Onie refused to start a school."

Rounding her eyes and mouth, Sookie sent her question directly to the older woman. Correctly interpreting it as either surprise or *why*, Milly explained. "He works both as a freighter for the town and the sheriff. With Bailey's Meadow growing quickly, as well as the addition of a saloon to town, he makes more trips for goods and also has to spend more hours as a lawman."

Raising her fists, Sookie quickly popped them open and extended her fingers. Confused, Milly looked to Wren for an explanation.

"She's concerned that it's dangerous in that town. That's our sign for danger."

With one hand held in front of her palm down in a comforting gesture, their cousin reassured the sisters. "Not at all. I have visited it, you know, to interview this man."

Her face softened. "And to hold his sister's new baby. Remember, I matched the baby's parents."

Smoothly, her face changed to a no-nonsense expression. "Saturday nights have been known to grow rowdy. That's all."

Pinching the fabric of her skirt between her fingers with her right hand, Sookie made downward motions with her left one. Scrunching her brow, the older woman struggled to understand. After repeating the gesture, she gave up and settled her gaze on Wren.

"My sister wants you to understand that we only have these clothes left to us. Will they be sufficient?"

The lavender-scented hanky appeared again as their cousin dabbed at her eyes. "What would Roberta think? She certainly believed you would be provided for after her death."

"Father never mentioned to any of us that the business automatically went to his partner should he die. And the fact that the house and its contents were listed as property of that business stunned both of us."

Wren wiped her eyes with the edge of her skirt before continuing. "Why, Father's partner refused to let us even pack our clothes, saying they belonged to him. We insisted on taking a few things that were purely our own and Mr. Blakenship relented, but not about our dresses."

Their cousin clucked her tongue. "Extremely odd."

As before when she grew serious, Milly tapped her chin. "It bears looking into. For now, though, pack what you want to take with you. I plan to have both of you stay at my house in Boston."

Milly watched while the older sister raised both shoulders and held out her hands palms up. "Are you asking why?"

Sookie nodded and the older woman explained, changing her pleasant voice to a more business-like tone. "We must order traveling suits and purchase shirtwaists and skirts appropriate for a teacher and her assistant."

While her sister grinned a relieved smile, Wren giggled. "Are you our fairy godmother?"

A sad, faraway look clouded Milly's face. "No, just a woman who loved your mother and wants to honor her in this way."

The little woman lifted the blue piece pinned to her mauve jacket. Suspended from a fleur de lis that also sported the same lovely blue lacquer as the piece attached to it, Sookie watched Milly open the face of her watch. Having grown up with luxuries, she recognized it immediately as a piece created by Patek Philippe and knew her mother's cousin must be financially well off. Very few people could afford this maker's keyless watches. The fact eased her mind about letting the woman buy them clothing.

"Oh my! That carriage will be here any minute. Hurry along girls and gather up what you want." Brushing her hands in the air to get them moving, Milly stood from the chair. She put hands to each of their backs when the sisters stood and gently pushed them out of the room.

No doubt about it. Sookie recognized in Milly Crenshaw a woman who made things happen. Could she actually make her prayer for a home and classroom come true? After a series of humiliations these last months, it seemed too much to hope.

Sighing, she hurried to her bedroom even as someone knocked on the scarred front door. Milly headed to it while she urged once more, "Hurry!"

Yes, this woman definitely enjoyed arranging the lives of others!

Over the next two weeks, Sookie realized how true that thought was. While both sisters were pampered and gifted with lovely clothing, she chaffed at the delay. Dread over her fiancé's reaction to her muteness created nightmares. It grew bad enough that Wren slept with her each night. Her sister woke her when she gave out her strangled cries, making those odd gurgling noises that strained her throat and caused her pain in the morning.

As badly as she dreaded it, Sookie knew she needed to head to Nebraska. Whatever future lay ahead of her there must be faced. Soon.

The Offices of The Emporium
Arnolds Corners, Massachusetts
Late April 1871

The man slammed clenched fists onto the desk. One sheet of paper would keep him alive. Where was it?

So far, O'Connor accepted his excuses and refrained from sending his thugs. Threats from the crime boss arrived almost daily. Notes carried to him by one grubby child after another demanded the money owed to the dangerous man.

Worse than the threats were the hunger and nervous energy eating at him. O'Connor refused to let him enter the gambling house. Him! Imagine the seedy boss refusing a gentleman and businessman like Silas Blakenship.

He needed to pay the man off and quickly. More than wanting to stay alive and healthy, Silas craved the poker tables. He knew the very next time he sat in on a game he would win. That belief pressed him to find a way to satisfy O'Connor.

Desperate, he even visited a few of the taverns along the river. No one would speak to him much less let him join a game of poker. O'Connor's Pleasure Palace was his only hope to prove he would win the next time he played.

Determined to find the deed he needed, Silas stood and moved each painting hung on the walls in his dead partner's office. Perhaps Donaldson attached it to the back of one. Last night he did the same thing to every painting and decoration in his new house. The house he illegally seized from the dead man's pathetic daughters.

Remembering how he refused to let them take their clothes brought a high-pitched giggle bubbling out of Silas's overly plump lips. How he hated those girls. Their father should have listened to reason and let him marry the oldest one, the teacher. His current problem would not exist if he were married to her.

As he lifted the last picture from the wall nearest the door, the portal opened a crack. A face hesitantly appeared around it. Silas glowered at the young man, He seemed to be always watching him since Donaldson's fatal accident.

"Mr. Blakenship, can I help you? Perhaps you want me to find something for you?"

Mr. Shasta, the office clerk, wrinkled his nose slightly when he glimpsed the painting Silas held. "Or should I summon the designer? She can do as well decorating your office as she does when arranging the window-front decorations for the store."

He scowled at the clerk. *Remember, you're the boss. None of them know what you did.*

"I need Donaldson's legal papers."

The young man scowled briefly and then worked hard to control the look. Even so, Silas glimpsed the fleeting expression of disapproval. Once he found everything necessary to control Donaldson's money and property, Shasta would be out on his rear. Silas could not stand anyone's laughter or disapproval.

Donaldson should not have laughed when Silas asked to marry the daughter. Oh, Silas still would have arranged the accident. Only, the man should not have laughed.

Squaring his shoulders, the clerk bravely suggested, "Could it be that the papers are in his house?"

Silas's face turned a deep red. Growling, he pointed a chubby finger on his free hand toward Shasta. "*My house*. And I've already looked, of course!"

The clerk bobbed his head once and began backing through the doorway. He moved too slowly for Silas to miss the expression on the man's pinched, disapproving features. Shasta knew something!

At the other's hesitation, he barked a command that sent his own voice up several octaves. He hated doing that. Hated the feminine sound to his voice at times like these.

"Stop! Tell me what you know about Donaldson's papers."

Frozen outside the doorway, Shasta stiffened. When he leaned into the room, the man opened his mouth to speak. Silas sensed the denial he meant to say. A lie for sure.

"You'll be out of a position today if you don't tell me the truth!"

The young man's chin lowered as his lips turned down. "There is a lockbox at Grant's bank."

"Excellent!" Silas crowed a high-pitched exclamation of triumph. "Clean out your desk. You're fired."

"But I—" Shock left the clerk unable to finish his sentence.

"I no longer need you. Get out of my sight." Silas slammed the door as he dissolved into a fit of giggles. He would be back at the poker tables in no time.

Rushing from the office, the giddy man made his way to the bank. Since it lay only a block away, he waddled there in record time. Typically, he took his carriage everywhere, short distances or long trips. This time he simply could not wait for it.

Not long afterward, he sat staring across a wide mahogany desk at the bank president. "Key! What do you mean?"

Feeling the moisture on his lip, Silas Blakenship dabbed at it before it dripped down onto the few inches of facial hair that formed a beard up and down his wobbly jaw. Lifting the linen, he wiped beads of perspiration from his wrinkling brow. "Shouldn't you keep the key as your bank owns the boxes?"

Robert Grant leaned backward in his leather chair, steepling his hands. The posture hinted at a patronizing lecture in the making. Silas hated for anyone to instruct him or speak down to him.

Months before, Grant argued with Silas about the will and power of attorney the partner produced. The banker's arguments did no good. He either could not or had no desire to prove Silas's documents to be the fakes they were.

That wintry day in the prior November, Silas coldly wielded power over the banker. Power he exercised at that moment once more. Holding up a hand, he cut off the banker before he could speak.

"Fine. There's a key. Simply show me another so I know what it looks like."

Grant rose. He opened the door a crack and called for a bank teller. That young man came, left, and returned with a sample lockbox key. Without a word, the banker glowered at Silas and pointed. Finally, he arched his brow in silent question.

"That's all I need. I do hope for better help when I return with the necessary key." Silas tipped his wide nose up slightly and harrumphed. He made the sound to force his voice lower, keeping the higher pitches under control. "Otherwise, I may be forced to move my banking to another town."

Hours later, the contents of every drawer covered the floor of the elegant home. A few keys lay on the large oak desk of the study. None appeared small enough or the right shape to be the lockbox key.

Where did Donaldson hide it?

With no one looking, the pudgy man stomped his feet in a frustrated dance. His perfect plan worked up to this point. And the Pleasure Palace's tables crooned a welcoming song in his mind. He had to get to his Sirens.

Silas shuddered at his next thought. *Was the man or his wife buried with it? How will I manage to exhume the bodies?*

No, he must be practical. Someone had it. Words slipped from his lips and bounced off the high ceiling of the room.

"I bet it must be one of the daughters."

He needed to grab one of them. Donaldson called the younger one his "little bird". Well, Silas

42

would get rid of the older sister and discover what song the little bird might sing for him.

He had to find that key.

CHAPTER 3

Onie placed a kiss on his daughter's dark blonde head, hugging her against his long torso. She squeezed chubby toddler arms around his neck. Even active as she was each day, the child stayed chubby. With adorably round cheeks and flashing blue eyes, Letty drew attention wherever she went.

Thirteen months to the day, this little one surely stayed busy. Still, they learned to deal well with each other during the last two months. They had needed to.

Getting a mother for the girl took longer than Onie expected. Finally, though, the two waited at the Plattsmouth depot for his bride. Or at least he waited. The baby enjoyed the outing with no idea of what lay ahead for them.

At his kiss, Letty exuberantly tightened her arms around his neck. "Daddy!" She punctuated the word with a sloppy kiss on his closely shaven cheek.

Ruby's determination six weeks before to force father and daughter together had been spot on. Onie did not enjoy the extra work his girl added to his day. No matter how worn out he felt after a day of work and then an evening spent caring for Letty, his little girl made life sweet for him.

The only thing he struggled to catch onto was cooking. All the pots and pans in his kitchen were new since he burned up the old ones. Even when he followed Ruby's directions and had her watching over his shoulder, he still burned whatever he cooked.

Letty wiggled in his arms and pushed against his chest. "Down!"

Indignation rippled through her voice. Typically, she was sweet-tempered like her mother. At this minute, Letty's voice warned him that a tantrum might happen soon.

Considering her nap time happened around this time each day, he could understand. That didn't matter; he had to stop it before she got started.

"Now, none of that." He gently jostled her a bit in his arms to focus his daughter.

When he spoke again, Onie allowed his voice to take on a soft, secretive tone. "Let me sit down and tell you about the mother coming on the train."

His baby girl loved stories. Immediately, her eyes rounded as she plopped a chubby thumb into her rosebud mouth. Crystal blue eyes rounded while she focused on her father's face.

Onie settled onto a nearby black iron bench. With no train in sight, he prepared to entertain his daughter. Just this once it would be okay to voice his dreams of the perfect bride.

"The mother on the train is a little bit of a woman. She has soft, dark hair that she winds up into a bun at the back of her head." He twirled a finger in front of Letty's face to show her the motion of winding the hair. Mesmerized, the sleepy girl's eyes followed his finger.

"Your new mother will sing to you with her sweet voice and tell you bedtime stories." He smiled as he felt his daughter relax against his chest. "She'll bake cookies for you to have as a snack after your naps, and teach you to be a lady like her."

47

Letty's breathing slowed and deepened. His own body slumped slightly against the bench and relaxed as his baby slept. Probably, the noise of the train would wake her. For the first time in the last hour, he hoped it would be a while before his bride arrived.

However, not more than ten minutes passed when the whistle of a train sounded. Looking down the track, Onie spied an engine rounding the bend with a line of cars trailing it.

In the few minutes before it arrived at the station, the engineer sounded the whistle again. Letty jerked in his arms and sat up. Eyes frightened, she whimpered.

He patted her back through the soft sweater she wore. Spring might have arrived, but the April air held a nip to it yet. Onie crooned to her and Letty leaned against him. Her faith in him was absolute, something he did not take for granted. The past weeks were spent bonding to build that faith.

They stayed on the bench at the back of the platform. The train came to a stop with a great belch of steam and one more whistle. Railroad employees scurried to pull out carts for luggage, attempting to zig zag around passengers waiting to board and those wanting to greet new arrivals. The press of bodies filling the edge of the platform made Onie glad to stay where he was and wait.

While the engine pulled several cars, only two of them transported passengers. The rest carried freight. Onie would haul some of it to Bailey's Meadow.

He fixed his eyes on the car with the open door. A conductor motioned for the crowd to back away from the door as he set a small set of steps in place. Lifting a hand, he guided a tall, elegantly dressed woman from the train.

Something about the woman grabbed Onie's attention and would not let go. She made him wish he wrote something very different to Mrs. Crenshaw. Watching this new arrival, he longed for a tall, willowy woman rather than a petite wife. The lady's every movement captured the waiting groom's focus.

She smiled cupid-bow lips at the conductor as she gracefully tipped her head in thanks. As her foot moved to the safety of the platform, Onie caught sight of one slim, booted ankle. Not a glimpse of flesh and yet her ankle attracted him.

That flummoxed him. No woman ever grabbed his attention this way. No, he had been a love 'em and leave 'em kind of guy. At least until Alicia and he were forced to marry.

In the April sunshine, the woman's shiny blue traveling suit glimmered. It created a glow about her that enhanced the shine of her curly dark hair and ivory skin. All in all, the woman looked too perfect to be real, especially after traveling by train for possibly a long distance.

Another movement at the passenger car pulled his gaze from his statuesque goddess. A delicately boned, small woman in a soft pink outfit accepted the conductor's outstretched hand. She also moved gracefully, also had soft, dark hair. Nevertheless, she failed to capture his attention. Unhappily, he realized she fit the description he sent to the matchmaker.

Could this woman be his bride? Others left the train, but no one fit his written description as closely as the small bird of a woman.

With a sigh, he stood and pulled the paper from his pocket to unfold it. Holding up the name he earlier wrote on it, he waited for her to look his way. If she reacted, he would know she was his intended.

The taller beauty noticed first, pointing toward him while gesturing oddly to the pocket Venus. A nod from the shorter one started the two moving his way. Funny, but he just now realized these women traveled together. Especially strange since he expected only one woman.

When they stood in front of him, the small woman spoke while her companion offered him a shy, exquisitely sweet smile. With difficulty, he tore his gaze from that woman's face. He wanted to memorize it. Instead, he glanced at the small wren of a woman.

"You are Onyx Hastings from Bailey's Meadow?" Equal parts hope and fatigue gave her words a breathless quality.

Not answering immediately, he set Letty on the bench and refolded the paper. The girl cried, causing the tall woman to automatically hold her arms out toward the distressed child. When the girl shied away and cried harder, she stopped and slowly lowered those empty arms.

A born mother. Why did he ask for someone like the little woman who only stared at the sobbing child? Well, he could change things, could refuse to marry this small lady in front of him. Perhaps her companion wanted a husband.

His eyes drifted to her. As he glanced her way, he saw the curly-haired beauty spin one black-gloved finger in a circle and point at the other woman. The short woman nodded and spoke to pull his focus her way.

"I repeat, are you Onyx Hastings?" While she kept an impersonal smile on her well-formed lips, something in her tone hinted at annoyance.

His dark eyes flared with equal annoyance as he answered her. "Yes, ma'am. I certainly am."

Turning from her, he picked up Letty and made shushing sounds near her ear. Out of the corner of his right eye, he glimpsed the tall goddess's expression soften as she watched father and child. Ignoring the small woman, he focused on her.

"You like kids, ma'am?"

Her companion chirped an answer, not giving the woman he watched a chance to speak. "She certainly does. In fact, she told me she can't wait to be a mother."

Not commenting on her rude interruption, Onie faced the little woman. "I expect you're Susan Kay Donaldson?"

A movement of arms pulled his glance back toward the woman he admired. She held up her hands, palms out, and shook them from side to side vigorously. Seeing his gaze on her, she pointed at her chest and smiled warmly.

"I'm Renee Donaldson, her sister." The short woman patted her quiet companion's arm. "This is your intended bride and I am her sister. Please call me Wren."

One step and then another took him directly in front of a dream come true. The dream he hadn't known he wanted. Letty hid her face against his armpit when Susan Kay beamed a friendly smile at his daughter and reached a gloved hand out to touch the girl's cheek.

"She'll warm up to you. Give it a day or so and she'll never remember life before you were a part of it."

A slight sigh and then a short nod answered him. The woman met his eyes before blushing and lowering her gaze.

The short black net attached to the black hat crowning her almost black curls hid her expression from him. Everything obscured a good view of her face. Frustrated, he resented it. He wanted to know every idea and expression that flitted across those finely crafted features.

Allowing that the woman might be shy, he turned his eyes to the sister. "I didn't expect you, Wren. Are you staying with us or do you have a match waiting for you in the area?" Even as he spoke, Onie looked around the thinning crowd for her possible husband.

The only man remained, standing alone while he watched the women intently. He wore a seaman's cap that reminded Onie of men who worked in Boston's harbor. When the small man noticed Onie's gaze, he ducked his head and hurried through a small clutch of people standing outside the depot's lone building.

In the next moment, he dismissed the curiously out of place man and listened to his future sister-in-law. "No husband. I'll be Sookie's assistant when she teaches and her helper at home." The woman's firm tone warned him not to argue.

He nodded. "I expect you can sleep in Letty's room. That is if you don't mind the baby."

"Fine. As long as I have a bed and quiet at night, I don't care who I share a room with."

Something she said had him glancing at his intended as he asked, "Sookie? Is that your nickname?" Meeting his gaze, her shapely lips turned up at each corner as she gave a short nod.

Odd that she never speaks. Onie assumed her shyness nearly crippled the woman, as quiet as she was around him.

"I have a few crates to collect. You ladies have trunks?"

They spent the next minutes finding two small trunks. Onie directed a railroad employee to move several crates by hand cart to his waiting wagon. During it all, Sookie's gaze fixed on the baby.

Knowing she would refuse to go to a stranger, Onie set Letty on the floor below the wagon's bench. Removing his wool coat, he added his own brawn and easily loaded crates into the wagon box. From there, Onie thanked the man and shoved the crates forward to hug the back of the wagon's bench.

Dusting his hands, he felt a gaze on him and turned to meet Sookie's admiring eyes. Feeling like the king of the world, he grinned.

"Best go with the man to be sure he returns with your trunk."

The words held a happy lilt, one that sounded strangely foreign to his ears. When had he last felt truly happy? Proud and satisfied, yes. But not happy.

One by one, he loaded the trunks and helped the women onto the bench seat. Somehow, Sookie coaxed Letty into the crook of her arm. The two played some game with fingers and Onie paused to watch before he apologized.

"Sorry I couldn't bring a buggy. Had to pick up these crates." He shrugged. "Too, I figured my bride would arrive with a trunk."

At the word *bride*, red flags flew in Sookie's cheeks and she looked away. Catching her embarrassment, Onie spoke to Wren. "Your sister's quite the shy one, isn't she?"

The Donaldson women exchanged a look over Letty's head that left Onie confused. Almost as if they found his comment funny. Why would a shy woman laugh about it?

Was she silly in the head? If she was, it didn't matter. The woman was here and already bonding with his daughter.

He felt pleased that his bride managed to draw the girl close to her. Even if Letty only sat there so she could better see the busy town around them, it was a start. The two looked as natural together as milk and cream.

Theirs was an easier start than he was having with the woman. She stayed mute, not saying one word to him and avoiding his gaze. Frustrated, he tried another subject.

Looking down at her sitting close to him on the tight bench, he explained about their wedding. "My minister's out of town for a few days. I arranged for us to stop at a small church on the edge of Plattsmouth. The man's family will stand as witnesses."

Sookie tapped his arm lightly and pointed to her sister. When he looked to Wren and then back at her sister, the older one ducked her head and made a muffled sound near Letty's ear. As far as he could hear, the odd rasping had no actual words to it. Still, the little girl responded well, relaxing into the crook of his fiancée's arm.

Smiling at the scene, Onie nodded. "Sure, Wren'll be one of our witnesses. Maybe the preacher's wife'll be the other."

For some strange reason, Sookie's satisfied smile had him feeling ten feet tall and about eighteen-years-old. She quickly turned her face downward to continue watching the sleeping girl. A slim white hand, no longer gloved, ran admiring fingers over the dark blonde curls clinging to the baby's forehead.

Her gesture reminded him of Ruby. His sister possessed a natural inclination to be a mother. She certainly mothered both him and their sister before taking on a stepson and Letty. Now she had baby Joy. These days, Ruby glowed with happiness.

He glimpsed a similar glow as he spied his bride out the corner of his eye. A tuneless humming came from her that stopped him cold. He remembered a few of his deaf students making that same sound.

"Sookie?" As an experiment, he softly whispered her name. The woman immediately looked his way. She could definitely hear.

At the question on her face, he scrambled for something to say. "Is Sookie a combination of Susan and Kay? At least the first part of Susan, maybe?"

Gifting him with a wide smile on her cupid bow lips, warmth stirred in his chest. Only a smile and she could make him happy. What would it be like when she finally spoke to him?

He hoped she got over this shyness quickly. And how would she teach school if she was this shy? Suddenly, he wanted to forget about that requirement if it made her less than a perfect match for him.

The small white building gleamed in the afternoon sunshine. Its door stood open, either to welcome them or simply to air out the church. He imagined the building remained shut up much of the week.

As far as churches went, this one was bare bones. It possessed no steeple or stained-glass windows. Inside was a small pump organ and a simple wooden altar standing in front of a handful of pews. The old minister and his wife stood at the front as they watched him lead in his intended. Wren, holding the sleeping child, followed behind.

"Welcome!" The minister's voice boomed. His small wife laid a hand to his arm and pointed at the sleeping baby. He nodded and gave them an apologetic smile.

In a softer voice, he continued. "Seems this promises to be the quietest wedding I've performed in my years."

Looking from one to the other, he asked the couple, "Are you both willing?"

Heads bobbed in unison. Smiling, the man lifted his bible from the altar to start the ceremony. "Typically, my wife would play the organ to add music to the occasion. With—" He waved his hand at the small sleeping form. "Well, I think we need to forego that part of the ceremony."

Sookie nodded her agreement while Onie grunted. The minister began the ceremony, reading the fifth chapter of Ephesians. The verses about wives submitting and husbands loving sounded vaguely familiar. Years had passed since Onie attended church, though he considered the only preacher in Bailey's Meadow to be his minister.

At the correct moment, after Preacher Miller chanted the expected list of "Will you cherish, honor" and so on, Onie softly whispered, "I do."

The man turned his focus to Sookie. Asking her to pledge her love, fidelity, and submission, the minister paused to hear the same vow from her. Onie waited too, knowing he would experience her voice washing over him. He expected it to be low and musical for some reason.

She met the old preacher's eyes and bobbed her chin. He frowned. "My dear, I need to hear your answer."

From behind, Wren softly explained. "She can't speak, Reverend."

Sadness clouded the man's eyes. "Well, then I now pronounce you man and wife."

Looking at Onie's thunderstruck expression, the old preacher made a doubtful offer. "You may kiss her if you are so inclined."

CHAPTER 4

If he was so inclined? Sookie searched her memory and was sure no other preacher ever ended any wedding she attended that way. It robbed her of the little joy she felt at this hurried marriage.

Onie eyed her warily, like a mad dog he needed to carefully observe. One he wanted to pet but feared. He showed no wariness in the wagon. Why should her muteness upset people like this? The expression on his face was all too familiar to her.

If any happiness remained about her wedding, her groom's dark frown erased it. He threw an accusing gaze first at Wren and then her. Hands on hips, he shook his head from side to side.

"I don't want a mute wife. Undo it, Preacher."

Shock caused the preacher's eyes to round behind his spectacles. "Didn't you hear the words, 'In the sight of God'?"

That man shook his head sadly. "You've joined yourself to her and best make the most of it. Many a man would be glad of this woman as his wife, mute or not. Even I can see kindness and goodness radiating from her."

Grumbling, Onie lifted the steel pen from the altar and jabbed it into the small pot of ink. He scrawled his name on the license. Looking at his bride, those snapping blue eyes took on the look of a sky filled with gathering thunder clouds as he all but dared her to sign the certificate.

Her slim fingers held only the smallest of tremors as she reached for the pen, brushing his. At the thrill of awareness and something more that shivered inside her, the bride's eyes widened. Her groom's dark blue gaze changed from anger to a sort of speculation. Experimentally, he reached under her short veil to run a finger over her blushing cheek. When electricity raced through her at his touch, he grinned a wolfish look.

Her eyes pleaded with him. Dark eyes in the dimness of the church's interior. Her well-shaped lips parted slightly, deepening the draw he felt a minute ago when he touched her.

"Maybe I will take that kiss now."

While the pen dripped, he leaned down to press his mouth to hers. Lips that started out soft increased their pressure. He made her forget everyone around them, and she jumped guiltily when the pastor cleared his throat pointedly.

"Mrs. Hastings, if you would sign?"

She looked down at the ink blots decorating their marriage certificate and knew those would forever remind her of her first kiss. Hastily, she signed the document, changing her name from Donaldson to Hastings. Laying aside the pen, Sookie smiled a satisfied grin in her husband's direction.

He waggled his head as if to clear it and focused on her. Catching her shy, embarrassed gaze, Onie tossed her a predatory grin. The grin of a hunter with prey in his sights. The smile was new to her, never seeing that look directed at herself. Her frown showed her struggle to understand exactly what it meant.

What did he want? That almost feral grin hinted at him viewing her as nothing more than a body that attracted him. She needed this man to accept her as a wife and want to learn to communicate with her.

After that odd grin, Onie helped the women out of the church and onto the bench seat. The trip to Bailey's Meadow began dismally. Communicating with his wife seemed the last thing that her new husband was interested in as he hunched gloomily next to her.

A light rain landed on his head and shoulders, deepening the morose mood. Dark brows, so odd with his light brown hair, lowered and his forehead creased. Those two matched his downturned lips.

Though Sookie sneaked occasional glances at him from under the tarp she held over herself and the baby, most of her attention focused on Letty. Amazingly, the child slept through the brief ceremony, not even waking when Wren passed her up to the new mother before Onie also lifted that woman into the wagon.

The child wore a lovely dress with smocking across the front. Rosebuds decorated her sweater, obviously done by a talented and loving hand. Who cared for her before the sisters' arrival?

The soft hair teased Sookie's caressing fingers. At her touch, the baby sighed in her sleep. Letty was young enough that she would quickly bond with Wren and her new mother. Such a pleasure to have a baby to nurture, even if she would spend time away from her to teach.

Her caressing fingers also stayed busy *talking* to her sister. The signs flew between them as Sookie tried to soothe Wren's fears. Onie's continued silence only intensified her worry.

"Can she hear?" The deep voiced stopped Sookie from signing. Her hands under the cover dropped to the little one in her lap.

Wren opened her mouth to answer, yet Sookie held up a palm to silence her. She turned, meeting her husband's eye. Her deliberate nod accompanied the arching of one finely shaped dark brow.

"I see that you can. That's a relief. I was pretty sure you could."

He hummed a moment. "I used signs with my students. My father sent me to France to learn it."

Sookie met his gaze when he paused. She felt her face tighten into a frown. Was she supposed to be impressed by his experience?

"How about I teach you sign language?"

Hands and fingers flew as Sookie signed in the direction of Wren. The sister nodded. Worry creased that one's brow and she met Onie's waiting eyes.

"My sister thanks you, but she has her own language. In fact, she wants to gift you with a dictionary of her signs when we arrive at your home."

Wren stifled a giggle. "She wants you to know that, as she is a teacher, she will be happy to instruct you in them."

The bridegroom snorted and gave his new wife a measuring glance. "A dictionary, huh? Even have it in book form?"

Rapid hand gestures passed between the women before Wren explained. "While Sookie convalesced, we created signs and wrote them down. Our mother's cousin, Mildred Crenshaw, paid to have the document turned into a small book."

Next, Wren's finely boned face tipped downward in a challenge. "We already have copies for the children at school and plan to stick with the signs we use daily."

Onie shook his head from side to side. "She's a teacher. She should use an established form of signing."

"But this is Sookie's way to communicate. Not something you can dictate, sir, even though she's now your wife."

Wren's throaty voice hissed out the challenge, loud enough to disturb Letty. The baby's head lifted, looking first toward her new aunt's dark frown. Seeing a stranger, an angry one, she wailed.

Sookie clicked her tongue. Putting her mouth next to the baby's ear, she made soothing noises. Letty looked to her father who smiled reassuringly. All the while, her new mother rubbed that small back in a circular pattern. Then Letty reached chubby arms toward her father.

"Daddy!"

Onie shook his head. "No."

When she again reached those arms up to him, he patted her head tenderly. "Stay on Mama's lap, baby girl. You're fine."

Onie crooned the words to Letty. With a last whimper, she relaxed into Sookie's arms and plopped a thumb into her rosebud mouth. All the while, she stared at Wren warily.

Those few words from Onie lifted a heavy stone off Sookie's chest. *Mama's lap.* He meant to keep her. Otherwise, her husband would have referred to her as something else. Maybe as *the nice woman's lap.* What mattered was that he said it.

Red faced at upsetting the baby, Wren's strangled tone when she spoke again hinted at her restraint. She was angry and wanted to spare Letty from any more fright. "About the sign language?"

With one finger, Onie tipped back his black felt bowler. His gaze traveled from his wife to her sister. "Tell me why she's mute."

Haltingly, Wren forced the story past her trembling lips. "We hate thinking about it, even six months after the accident happened. Our parents and Sookie took the family's carriage that day to visit a sick friend of our family. Even months later, she and I don't know what happened to cause the accident."

Shrugging, Wren broke off. Breathing deeply and slowly, the young woman worked to control her sorrow. At her side, Sookie's hands flew. Her sister nodded.

"While our parents both perished, Sookie emerged from the accident with a terrible wound. A piece of the vehicle broke loose to lodge in her throat." As Wren spoke, her sister's fingers touched the burning scar through her high collar.

"Will she heal and recover her voice?" Hope and sadness mixed to make Onie's voice low and soft.

A shake of his wife's curly head answered him. Wren squeezed her sister's arm tenderly and offered an explanation. "There doesn't seem to be any hope of that. She is able to very, very softly make a few sounds. You probably noticed her put her mouth to the baby's ear."

At the man's nod, Wren explained. "She hums songs and can make soothing noises for her. Even that causes her discomfort."

Onie's horrified voice caused his bride to lower her brows as her lips pinched with displeasure. "Don't do it then. It's not worth hurting you."

Sookie tapped her chest at the same time as she touched Letty. Wren interpreted the motion. "That means *mine*. Letty is her baby now."

Onie secured the reins temporarily under his left thigh. Sitting on them, he touched his chest and Sookie's shoulder. She sagged with relief at the message.

They were married for good. Why he accepted an imperfect woman like her mystified Sookie? Just looking at the man told her he had more than his share of pride. How could he be proud of a damaged wife?

His deep voice rumbled near her as he took up the leathers again. "Imagine the two of you inventing your own language. Must have taken a lot of creativity."

Sookie lifted a finger and touched the invisible numbers on a make-believe clock. "She says time. It took a lot of time."

Wren sighed. "We had a great deal of time since Sister couldn't work and I stayed home from school to nurse her."

"Are you still in school?"

Shaking her dark-brown hair, Wren explained, "I graduated, doing most of my work from home. My teachers sent lessons to me so I wouldn't fall behind."

Face serious, her brother-in-law nodded. "Good enough. I expect helping your sister will be temporary. You'll be wanting to go to normal school or a women's college."

Wren's head moved from side to side. "No money for that since our parents' death."

"But your clothes—"

Sookie circled her face with a finger and then made an M in the air, her sign for Cousin Milly. Onie's curious eyes looked to Wren.

"Cousin Milly bought clothing for us. She found us in terrible poverty since Father's business partner inherited everything, our home and clothes included."

Onie's shoulders stiffened as he scowled. "Now that sounds fishy. Did Mrs. Crenshaw look into the matter?"

Wren fidgeted with the lacy ruffle under her chin. "She started an inquiry. I'm sorry, but I don't know any details."

Buildings replaced the endless prairie. While the wood of the shops on the main street were painted, here and there some wood showed the start of weathering. Sookie wondered at the town's age. Not new, but it must be only a few years old.

They passed a mercantile advertising paint and hardware. Next came a livery where a large man waved a hand to greet them. Sookie admired the lovely white house she glimpsed behind that business. The wagon rolled on, not giving her much of a chance to see it, and finally they stopped at a building with a sign proclaiming *Hastings Freight*.

Making what looked like a peaked roof with her index fingers, Sookie flapped her right hand out with the palm up. She nodded at Wren and then stuck her chin in Onie's direction. Her sister returned the nod.

"My sister wants to know why we stopped here instead of your house."

The bride's heart sank at his answer. "I built a few rooms at the back of the business and live there."

The rectangle hooked onto his warehouse housed a long room that combined both the kitchen and parlor. Touring the inside, she discovered two bedrooms. The smaller of the two held a crib and a narrow bed. A larger bed clearly told Sookie where Onie slept.

Bare walls and the lack of curtains tugged at Sookie's emotions. Really, the man did need a wife. Letty should grow up knowing how a cozy home looked. She and Wren would be busy each evening sewing. That is, if her husband could afford the fabric.

Pulling the pins from her broad-brimmed hat, she removed it from her hair. Pushing in a few loose pins, she patted the low pompadour that fitted neatly under the hat. She longed for a mirror, but her husband did not have one of those either.

Wren removed her hat also, letting Letty hold it to finger the silk peonies that decorated the crown. The little girl tried to put it on her own head, missing several times. With a giggle, Wren helped her and then said how pretty she was.

Onie came through the door, pushing their trunk on a dolly. "Don't want to crowd my—our bedroom. How about I put this by the room's door here?" He wheeled the trunk to the wall by the door.

Sookie nodded with an easy smile. As long as she had her things, she was happy. Wren looked up and shrugged before returning to the game of peekaboo she played with Letty using the hat as a sort of shield.

"May I come in?"

A friendly call preceded a tall woman who walked into the kitchen part of the long room, carrying a casserole dish. She set it on the stove and then opened the oven door. Tsking at the cold stove, she used a towel to pull out the drawer at the bottom. First stirring the coals, she added a small stick of wood.

Wiping her hands on the towel, she laid it back on the edge of the sink and looked around. Shiny chocolate hair neatly lay against her head and was secured in a large bun at the nape of her neck. Even though the woman was older than Onie and had brown eyes instead of dark blue, Sookie saw the resemblance to her husband.

She crossed her fingers at Wren and then pointed between the woman and Onie. Wren shrugged, opening her lips while she made a tumbling motion from them with one finger. Suddenly, both women pinkened as they felt every eye in the room on them.

Almost every eye. Letty ignored her new mother and aunt to race to the woman, wrapping her arms tightly around that one's legs. This answered the question of who cared for her before Sookie's arrival.

"Hello." Gentle and friendly, that word started a churning inside Sookie, stirring up sorrow. She badly wished she could answer.

"Ruby, this is Sookie. And the shorter woman is Wren, my bride's sister." The visitor glanced between them with a welcoming smile.

Onie pointed at the woman. "And this is my sister, Ruby Kline."

His sister waited. When neither woman broke the awkward silence, Onie added, "Sookie signs. She can't speak because of an injury."

Not missing a beat, his sister faced Onie and asked, "What is the sign so I can say hello?"

Like any younger brother who once was a pest, he clucked his tongue. "Don't you know anything? I said that she can't speak. I didn't say she was deaf."

"Don't get huffy with me, Onyx Hastings! How will I know if she says hello to me?"

Stepping between the siblings, Sookie met the woman's dark gaze and waved. Ruby gave a silvery laugh. "That's easy enough to understand."

By that time, Wren had the trunk unlocked. She drew out a small book and offered it to Ruby.

"Lovely to meet you, Mrs. Kline. Please take this book that explains Sookie's signs."

"Ruby, please. And may I call you both by your first names?"

At their nods, Onie's sister gave each a gentle, welcoming smile. Sookie privately thought that she'd never met another woman who oozed motherly nurturing.

"This little book is quite impressive. I imagine the room in the left margin is so a person can draw the signs."

The two sisters nodded. "Or Sookie can draw them for a person who isn't understanding."

"There is even room left at the back of the book to add new signs as we create them." Enthusiasm caused Wren to speak quickly, pulling a tolerant, kind smile from the older woman who looked at the book with her.

"Our cousin, Mildred Crenshaw, paid to have the books printed. She thought it would help Sookie communicate with her students."

Interest sparked in the other woman's eyes. "I know Mrs. Crenshaw. She matched me with my husband."

Ruby tapped her lips. "In fact, our sister is married to her godson."

As they watched, Sookie put her index fingers about two inches apart and then turned her hand in a circle with one of those fingers pointing down. Ruby giggled, causing both sisters to smile. No one could be offended by this loving woman.

"She says it's a small world. And I agree since this seems to be quite a family coincidence."

"Perhaps. Mrs. Crenshaw knows what she's about when matching people, so I know Sookie is meant to be here." She patted Wren's shoulder. "And you, too."

A tendril of dark hair slipped along with a pin as Wren nodded. "Yes, I'm Sookie's classroom helper."

At the mention of school, Onie frowned. "We'll need to have a town meeting. Since my wife can't speak, I want to be sure parents will want her as the teacher."

"Ezra and I will support her. I can't see any reason not to have her teach Frank."

"Well, that's one student. How about the others? And we need to decide when to start."

He slapped his bowler against one thigh in thought. "No, a meeting has to happen."

Later, from somewhere, Sookie remembered that in the West people called the evening meal supper rather than dinner. Perhaps it was in one of the dime novels she and Wren read before starting the trip to Nebraska. No matter where, the newly formed little family sat down to eat the potato casserole Ruby brought them.

Ruby herself had hurried home to nurse her small baby. "And my boys, too."

The woman laughed as she added that. Contentment glowed on her face. Cousin Milly did well with that woman's match.

Sleep during the trip had been grabbed in snatches. Letty and Wren both went to bed early that night. Sookie felt that same draw to sleep. Only, she had the awkward situation of sharing her bed. Or, more accurately, *his* bed.

With slow, heavy movements, she pushed her body to keep working. One by one, she moved clothing from the trunk into bureau drawers. Onie cleared two for her so she had plenty of room.

Neither sister had a great deal of accessories. Milly would have been more generous but Sookie stood firm with the woman, saying they each needed only a church dress, a traveling suit, and two decent everyday dresses. Two petticoats, chemises, and three sets of lacy drawers for each woman came along with those outer items. Milly kindly also provided two linen nightdresses. Plenty from a kind woman who loved helping others.

Sookie's hands itched to unpack her sister's clothes as well. It would give her an excuse to stay up longer. Doing that would mean entering the small bedroom where Letty and Wren slept, possibly waking them. Sighing, she left the remaining clothes in the trunk.

Looking up from the book of sign's that he studied, her husband flashed his flirty grin. Only this time, the arch of one brow and the spark in his blue eyes hinted at a playful side to his nature.

Mischievous! That was the right word, she thought.

"Are you done?" Onie spread his large hands apart with their palms down while he asked the question, showing Sookie's sign for *done*.

Frowning, she pointed to her chest and then put a finger to her ear. He nodded. "I know you can hear. I wanted to practice the sign so you would know I understand you."

Warmth flooded her. Not the tingling warmth from Onie's touch. This happy feeling came from his desire to communicate with her and accept her disability. One of her wishes in a husband was coming true, as if Cousin Milly really were a fairy godmother sending Sookie to her prince.

Setting aside the book, Onie rose and crossed the small room to stand near Sookie and the trunk. Near the bedroom, also. He touched a finger to his chest and then one on her cheek. "Mine." Her breath came in short pants at her nervousness as he claimed her.

Finished signing, he picked up her hand and turned it palm up. With slow movements, he traced that palm with one finger, tickling his wife. Zings of electricity flew between them. It surprised Sookie that none flashed bright in the air. The sensations pulsed, incredible and strong.

Without words, Onie led her through the doorway and into the bedroom. What passed put to rest any fears Sookie still had about her husband sending her away or annulling the marriage. Not after the two became one.

CHAPTER 5

People crowded into the pews of the small church. Wren and Sookie sat at the front, not circulating to meet anyone. Both wore their new church dresses, something that added to Sookie's anxiety. Onie told both women to stay in their seats and only greet the people who came to them. He wanted to hold them apart for a reason Sookie struggled to guess.

Onie also warned Wren not to sign. Not that he wanted them to stay quiet. No, he urged them to carry on a conversation with only Sookie signing her side of the interaction.

"I want people to see you signing and hearing." That much he did explain.

Curious, Sookie looked around at the small crowds and the building itself. One aisle ran up the center. On each side of that stood short pews, only long enough to seat three adults comfortably.

Already, pews were crammed tight. Some with even four adults. Others with adults holding children on each knee. As small as the town was, she marveled at the number of people who packed into the church to discuss a school.

No, they were there to discuss the school's teacher. Children raced up and down the aisle, waiting for the meeting to start. Several darted up to the front pew and peeked around it to see the strange woman who concerned their parents.

Grabbing a stolen glance, they often raced off giggling. As if they braved facing a dragon or some wild beast and won. It left her in no doubt of what the parents said at home before the meeting.

Sookie covered her eyes. Understanding, Wren grabbed her sister's hand and gave it an encouraging squeeze.

"I know you don't want to face this. You do want to teach again, though. Right?"

The older sister stacked imaginary blocks one after another with her hands in front of her chest. At

Sookie's sign for *very much*, Wren gave a short, satisfied nod.

"Well then. We sit here and wait for Onie to make that happen."

Unbidden, a dreamy sigh struggled past Sookie's lips. Wren giggled at hearing it. Her former role as a teasing younger sister reared its head, a role she formerly put aside after Sookie's injury.

"Your prince will perform an act of bravery for his lady." She teased her older sister and giggled louder when that woman's face flamed.

From her spot on the floor, Letty looked up at the sound of her aunt's laugh. The little one grinned, showing two small front teeth. From the drool on her chin, Sookie knew the baby would soon have a third tooth.

Such an easy child to care for and love. After two days, Letty already showed a preference for her mother over Wren or even Ruby. It made Sookie feel as if she were a puzzle piece fitted into its exact spot. A spot only she could fill.

Mr. Bailey, the mercantile owner, walked to the front of the church. Sookie knew the man by sight since she met him her first full day in the town when she bought foodstuffs to fill Onie's empty cupboards. Her husband sheepishly admitted that Ruby sent most of the food he and Letty ate. She remembered his embarrassed shrug as he admitted, "Cooking's the only thing I've never been able to learn."

That suited her fine. It meant he needed her for more appetites than the one he appeased in the dark. An appetite he satisfied for both of them very nicely, making her already half in love with him.

The mayor's movements pulled Sookie's mind from her very private and scandalous memories. Standing at the small podium, he raised his hands to signal the start of the proceedings. Children settled on laps or jammed into tightly packed pews. An anxious quiet fell across the room.

"Folks, we've gained ourselves a teacher."

"Aye," he paused and pointed at Sookie. "She's a good un. Been teaching years in the East."

A sly grin crossed the Irishman's face. "What be good enough for them in the East be good for our own kiddies, I'm a thinkin'."

A chorus of cheers and even one "Amen" sounded. Bailey raised his hands once again to silence the crowd. "Only, there be one wee trouble. The teacher be mute."

For many, this only confirmed the gossip they heard after Sookie's visit to the mercantile. No gasps of surprise came to her ears. Only grumbling and murmurs sounded across the room.

"Now, I'm believin' this ken work. Why, ye ask?"

He stopped and stared meaningfully at people seated in different spots in the church. "Ezra Kline says it will be foine. Be ye knowin' when that man's been wrong? Nay, not ever."

Onie stood from a chair in a spot behind the podium. Ezra also rose to follow his brother-in-law forward. Bailey shook hands with both men and headed for one of the empty chairs.

"You all know I trained as a teacher."

Onie's low voice, filled with confidence and energy, rose to the ceiling and bounced down again on the crowded church. "I and my wife have a plan for how she will teach your children."

Townspeople leaned forward in their seats. A few anxious gasps displayed how badly these people wanted to have a teacher. Wanted this to work.

"My wife speaks through signs, gestures your children will easily learn. And learning them will teach language and grammar. In the end, they will be more skilled speakers and writers."

One man popped up. Concern tightened his voice as he spoke. "But my littlest ain't ready fer that kind of learnin'. What about him? How will he understand his teacher?"

Onie motioned with his palms down to calm the man. "Children love games. Learning the signs will be like a game for the littlest ones. And my wife will know how to make it work that way."

A woman holding a baby and another child clutching at her calico skirt rose. Her face showed equal parts interest and apprehension. Watching her,

Sookie sensed how badly this woman and others around her wanted this to work.

"Tell us how she'll do that." A chorus of agreement rippled across the congregated group.

Onie bobbed his head. Looking silently at the gathered people, he finally focused his gaze on the woman who remained standing. "Teaching nursery rhymes is one way she intends to start. With her sister's help, the smaller children will learn the rhymes. Then signs will be substituted for words in the rhymes to help the children remember what they mean."

The standing woman smiled. A broad, warm expression that beamed her acceptance of the new teacher. She nodded and sat again.

The mayor returned to the podium. Slapping Onie on the back, he took over the meeting. Sookie noticed the lack of tension now in that man's shoulders. Obviously, Onie convinced him also.

"Well, folks? I be happy to start me kiddies into the school."

Murmurs of agreement sounded. "Onie got us two for the cost o' one teacher. Her sissy'll be helping each day without costin' us a penny more."

Turning her head, Sookie glimpsed many smiles directed her way. Poking Wren to turn, they smiled back at the people. Teaching would be doubly hard since the kids needed to be taught the signs. No matter, she once again possessed a classroom.

Or did she?

Mayor Bailey continued speaking. People had risen, thinking the meeting over. His raised hands and loud voice stopped them.

"Aye, a foine thing. But we be needin' to know fer sure. So, we'll have the teacher workin' for a month's trial."

Was this Onie's idea? Sookie's face searched out his. His nostrils flared with anger. As she watched, he fisted his hands. Otherwise, his expression remained as it had been. She saw enough to know her husband did not scheme with the mayor to create this trial period.

Disregarding Onie's instructions to stay in the pew, Sookie picked up Letty and stood. Wren rose also and waited at her sister's elbow. They both faced the crowd.

Unable to sign while holding her daughter, Sookie kissed Letty's forehead and handed her to Wren. Before the baby left her arms, she softly patted her mother's cheeks and babbled sounds that only Letty herself understood. The sight brought happy sighs from many gathered there.

Hands flew as Sookie *spoke* to the group. Wren watched carefully and interpreted at Sookie's pauses. She did her best to reflect in the tone of her words what she saw on Sookie's face.

"My sister looks forward to meeting your children. Parents also, but mostly the children." Wren smiled sweetly. "I do as well. This will be a chance for me to decide if I want to attend a teacher college in another year."

En masse, the group rose and surged forward. Questions flew around them. *Was she born mute? Can the teacher hear? Will she recover her voice?* Sookie signed responses to each that Wren interpreted.

By the end of the evening, they met too many community members to recall most names. Their new teacher focused on identifying children's names, knowing each would receive a sign as her way of calling his or her name.

What would she assign to them? Children wanted to know, after Wren told them about it.

The few that stayed close by earned a *special name* from the gesturing teacher, one that Wren explained to them. Taps to an ear or on the cheek became part of this informal naming ceremony with children giggling happily. Parents beamed as well, satisfied with the evening's outcome.

Such a change from an hour before when no one approached the sisters. The welcome filled Sookie's heart. She felt like Bailey's Meadow became home to her as she left the church.

No wonder the shot, when it flew past and grazed her temple, came as a shock. She believed everyone in town happy now to have her there. The jarring trauma of it froze her in place.

Mayor Bailey pulled her back into the building. His yell for the sheriff confused her or maybe the graze from the bullet left her befuddled. Had she met a sheriff?

Out of slightly glazed eyes, she watched her husband run toward her. No other man approached. A fact nagged at her memory and finally surfaced. Her husband was the part-time lawman.

"What in the blue blazes happened?"

Onie focused on Bailey. His tone hinted at blame. Under it, she made out a barely controlled hint of fear.

"Heard a shot and pulled yer missus in. The wee lass wid yer babe in arms come in on her own. But our teacher took a hit."

Uttering an oath, Onie swept his wife up into strong arms. She sighed against his chest with relief. Giving up the struggle to appear fine, she sank back against him.

He stalked past the crowd at the door to lay her onto a pew It was too short to allow her legs to completely fit. When she tried to sit up after this change in position, he gently urged her down.

Growling softly, Onie's voice held a note of steel. "Stay there. Ruby's gonna look at your head."

Her sister-in-law loomed over her, smiling in her nurturing way to bring calm to the situation.

Sookie tried to return the expression. Before her mouth could tip upward, she spiraled downward in blackness.

Onie raced out of the church, shoving past shoulders crowding the doorway as people peeked out into the darkness with one lantern. He grabbed it from Mr. Sawyer, the owner of the town's first bank, and walked with Bailey to the spot Sookie stood only minutes earlier.

"The furrow on her temple was diagonal. I'm thinking we need to search the ground for the bullet if we want to know more about that shooter."

"Man, ought'n we be lookin' fer him wid the gun and not playin' on yon ground?"

"Nah. The shooter sat on the roof. I can imagine the path of the shot." Onie raised the lantern high. "Tomorrow, I'll look up there to see if he left anything."

On one knee, Onie stuck his penknife into the ground. Once. Twice. On the third attempt he hit something other than the give of soil around the blade. Digging with the knife, he produced a 50-caliber slug.

By the light he held, Onie showed it to Bailey. "Look familiar?"

Bailey's redhead nodded. "Heard tell the army's switched to the 1868 Springfield that uses such as that. Might be someone's got a trapdoor rifle, but why shoot yer foine missus?"

"Second time in a year that she's almost died." Onie furrowed his brow. "That is, I only know of two times. Might be more."

Another lantern bobbed out of the building. As it quickly neared, he recognized his sister. Searching beyond her, he saw Ezra carry Sookie. Wren hurried behind him, clutching Letty tightly.

Slipping the bullet into his vest pocket, he handed the lantern to Bailey. "Give that back to Sawyer for me, will you?"

Not waiting for a response, his long legs ate up the distance to his brother-in-law. Some strange mix of panic and anger churned inside him at the sight of another man's hands on his wife. Odd since he only met her two days before.

He only felt that way on account of her wound, he mentally assured. Still, he reached under Ezra's arms to snatch her away from the larger man. Clasped close to her husband's broad chest, Sookie's eyes briefly flitted open. At least she was sort of conscious.

This relieved him. Even so, his gaze strayed over his shoulder to peer once more at the roof of the church. Had the gunman seen clearly in the dark so that he recognized Sookie before shooting? What threat did she pose to someone to take this extreme action?

Ruby raced ahead of him. When he arrived at the backdoor to the rooms behind his warehouse, Ruby stood in the opening with welcoming light filling the room behind her. She waved a hand to beckon him inside.

"Hurry, Onie. She needs to lay flat and have that gash cleaned." He knew her tone well from his childhood. She acted as mother to him, and he rushed to obey her now just like he did in his youth.

Gently, he stretched her pliant form out on the bed. As he adjusted his wife's head on the pillow, she groaned an odd sound. He found it hard to tell what that meant since the injury distorted any sound she managed to produce. Watching the muscles tighten around Sookie's beautifully shaped mouth, he guessed pain gripped her.

"Ruby, have you got any willow bark tea ready for her?"

Strong hands grabbed his shoulders and turned him to look at the door. "Go on and do your sheriff thing. Your wife will be fine if you only let me take care of her."

In a less bossy tone his sister added, "You're in my way here."

In the kitchen, Wren fed Letty a slice of bread and butter. The little one chortled and held her snack high for her father to see. He ruffled her curls. The ghost of a smile flitted across his face as he looked down at his daughter before focusing on her new aunt.

"Think carefully. Has there been any other strange accidents or near misses in the last several months? Even before the carriage accident?"

Wren cradled her head, sitting stiff and silent. When she lowered her hands, the young woman bobbed her head. Understanding, belated realization, showed in her features.

"My family came down with a terrible case of food poisoning the week of the carriage accident. Mother was just barely well enough to go with Father and Sookie on the visit. If only she—"

Tears coursed over Wren's finely boned cheeks and dripped from the tip of her nose. Letty set the bread on the table and stared. "Daddy."

The word came out as a statement and not a question. Onie struggled to understand what the girl wanted. However, she seemed satisfied when he moved to place a reassuring hand on Wren's shoulder. Picking up her bread, the baby gummed it again.

"And after the accident? Think of anything she might have mentioned from her time at work or her travel to and from jobs."

His low voice pushed her to remember anything, something, a clue of some kind. He refused to believe tonight's attack was random. His intuition urged him to consider its connection somehow to the carriage accident.

Words from the day before rose to the front of his brain. He repeated them aloud for Wren, wanting confirmation. "Mrs. Crenshaw is looking into your inheritance, right? Your father's business, too?"

Swiping her face with a square of fine white linen, Wren met his gaze blankly. Dawning comprehension and horror widened her tear-filled eyes. "You think Sookie or both of us inherited something? Something Mr. Blankenship stole from us?"

"Blakenship? Who's that?" Onie searched his memory but could not recall the name.

"Father's partner in The Emporium. Quite a successful business." Pride warmed Wren's voice as she mentioned the store.

Onie gave a clipped nod of his chin. "Yeah, I think this Blakenship is up to his eyeballs in this. Must be your cousin's detective is getting close to something."

At his new sister's blank look, he explained. "The sniper took a chance tonight, shooting like that. Someone might have grabbed him getting off that roof." Two fingers traced his dimpled chin as Onie went on with his speculation. "I'm thinking he got a wire telling him to act quickly."

"Please, Onie. Wire the sheriff in Arnold's Corners and have Father's partner arrested."

Slowly his head shook from side to side. "It's not that easy. Suspecting and proving are two different things. Could be that the Mrs. Crenshaw's detective will find the proof."

"Can you ask about a telegram from Blakenship at the telegraph office?"

Approval beamed from his gaze. "Great idea. I doubt he'd use his real name, but I have an idea of how to find the gunman."

At Wren's confused stare, he waved his hand dismissively. "Never mind. I'll head to the telegraph office now. Might be a few details I can squeeze from Wiley Schwartz, our telegrapher."

About to leave, Onie paused. "That is, if you can handle Letty. Wash her and put her to bed for me?"

He waited and the young woman nodded. Smiling, she reached a finger out to tickle the baby. "We'll be fine. Go ahead."

Glad to have only his sheriff role to concentrate on at the moment, he plopped the felt bowler on his head and left. Walking in the dark bothered him that night. A spot between his shoulder blades itched as if the shooter might aim at him next, randomly shooting townspeople.

Occam's Razor applied here. The simpler answer had to be correct. That meant there was no deranged man shooting randomly. This connected with those earlier attempts to kill the Donaldson family. Was Wren also in danger?

Worse yet, would he lose another wife if he failed to discover the assassin's identity? Was it pride alone that refused to let that happen or was some buried emotion flaring to life?

Impossible after only one day together. Or was it?

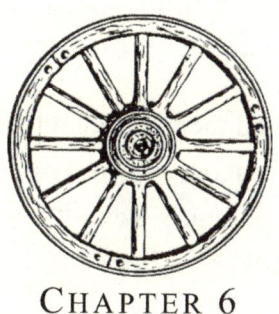

CHAPTER 6

"Telegrams are private, Hastings. You know that!"

Schwartz wrinkled his nose as if smelling rotten food and pulled on his suspenders. The mere idea of revealing details from telegrams repelled him. At least, that was the image he projected. The man put on a good act, only an act.

"Come on, Wiley. You love gossiping about news you learn in them. I've heard you, over a whiskey in Crawford's saloon, say more than one piece of gossip from wires."

The face across from his wrinkled tighter until only small pig eyes stared at him with loathing. "I never done that!"

Onie waved a hand dismissively. "Doesn't matter. All I care about is catching the guy who tried to kill my wife."

The scrunched face unfolded like a sponge released from someone's grip. His small eyes doubled in size at Onie's news. "I been here all night. Didn't hear 'bout that."

He narrowed those eyes again speculatively. "She gonna be okay?"

Not sure if the man wished Sookie well or wanted sensational news about her, Onie gave a dismissive shrug. "About those telegrams. You get any really short ones in the last day or two. Maybe even only one word."

Schwartz moved from the counter to the small room's desk where the telegraph sat. He leafed through papers and pulled one from the stack. Back at the counter, he laid it down and stabbed it with a beefy finger.

"This one were odd. It only said, 'Now'." His triumphant grin contradicted the note of confusion his voice held while he described the telegram.

"Sounds like what I'd expect. Who'd you take it to?"

"That were strange too. Man by the name of Smith, sleeping at Ezra's livery. Never known Ezra to let anyone sleep there."

With a shake of his head, Onie considered that. "He didn't mention anything to me about a vagrant or visitor. Wonder what's up."

With a backward wave of his hand to Schwartz he drifted from the office, deep in thought. Rather than burst into the livery looking for this Smith, he would visit Ezra. His brother-in-law may have noticed something about the man.

Smith. Just the name seemed suspicious. Using it was as good as admitting a man's name was false.

Making his way through the moonless night, Onie rounded the livery and headed for the white house. Its light paint glowed faintly in the darkness. No matter, he knew his way even if it were painted black and hidden from him in the night. He came often enough when his baby girl lived here with Ruby.

Knocking at the backdoor of the kitchen, he waited. No wonder it was taking his brother-in-law a while to answer. Ruby was still at Onie's house with Sookie. That meant Ezra was settling young Frank and baby Joy into bed on his own.

A curtain twitched allowing a flood of low lantern light to escape the house. A small face, made eerie by the light behind him, peered out. The small body loudly proclaimed, "It's Uncle Onie, Pa. I'm lettin' him in."

The turn of a key scraped in the quiet night. From inside the house, Joy bellowed her anger. Or was her cry due to sadness?

He lacked enough experience with babies to know the difference in their cries. With Sookie here, he would have a chance to learn. To do over what he missed with Letty.

That stopped him so that he only stared blankly at Frank when the five-year-old opened the door. He meant Sookie to be a convenience in his life and a teacher for the town. Suddenly, he saw the two of them as partners raising children? That thought hinted at how strongly he hoped for a future with her.

He took her to bed and now he dreamed of their grand future with one another? Strangely, he knew it as true. Seeing her limp and bleeding tonight halted his breathing. His stomach clenched in true fear at the possibility of losing her. That reaction alone told him the woman's appearance in his life two days earlier triggered a part of him that had been waiting for her. It almost made him believe in the providence of God.

"Uncle Onie?" The boy's voice grew small, holding a tiny bit of tremble to it.

Frank's face scrunched in concern. "You needin' my Pa? He can fix most everything that's wrong."

The boy's boast about his father brought Onie out of his stunned thoughts. He smiled and ruffled the boy's light brown, nearly blonde curls. A gift from his German ancestry and his true father. Or so Onie was told.

The months before, the wife of Frank's real father kidnapped the boy. After Ezra rescued him, Ruby helped explain about the reason. Without going into detail about procreation, Ruby did her best to explain about the other man who fathered the boy. When Frank learned that Ezra was somehow not his real dad, the boy denied it.

Onie remembered the anguish on his brother-in-law's face in that moment. Then Frank clung to Ezra's legs. The big man lifted him and the boy placed both hands on Ezra's cheeks.

"We been together always, Pa. I love you."

That moment cemented the bond amongst Ruby's small family. She confided to Onie that they still watched Frank, waiting for more questions about the man after whom his mother named him. In the months that followed, none came. Young Frank seemed to forget the kidnapping and anything he learned after it.

Stepping into the house, Onie grinned down at the boy. Frank wore his usual happy grin, no matter that his new aunt was nearly killed an hour before. Not much got that boy down.

"You wanna talk to Pa?"

"Yeah. He upstairs?" Onie looked upward as he said that.

Frank followed his gaze and nodded, curls bouncing against his forehead. He turned and ran from the room. Ruby would have kittens to see him running in the house. Onie knew that from his own childhood under his sister's supervision. Obviously, the boy was enjoying his mother's brief absence.

Ezra's deep voice boomed down the stairs. "I hear you running. Stop that, boy!"

Frank froze and threw a look of awe upward before gazing in his uncle's direction with wide eyes. "He knows everything."

Stifling a laugh, Onie kept silent. He could have explained about Ezra hearing the boy's fast steps on the wood floors. Doing that might put a dent in Frank's worship of his hero. Not for all the gold in Fort Knox would he do that to the boy.

Nodding, Onie patted Frank's shoulder, moving past him. One step after another led him up the stairs to the baby's room. Letty's old room before Ruby forced him to see what he missed by not having his daughter in his own home.

Right as always, and he marveled at her mother's wisdom. She invariably sensed what was right for him and their sister. Now she did the same with Frank, Letty, and the new baby.

One candle burned on the tall dresser. He peeked into the nursery. Ezra rocked the quiet baby. For the first time, Onie realized the baby lay silent, her cries only an echo in his mind.

With a finger of his free hand to his lips, the big man signaled for him to be quiet. He rose carefully, stepping lightly to the crib. Slowly, he lowered the swaddled bundle into it. All the while, both men halted their breathing.

On thick hobnailed boots, Ezra tiptoed from the small room. Onie backed away and the large man carefully closed the bedroom door. As one, the two men sagged against the wall outside her room when Joy stayed asleep through it all.

Waving for him to follow, his brother-in-law headed down to the parlor. Onie followed and sat across from Ezra with Frank on his lap. That one protested, "I'm not sleepy."

Not a moment later the boy cuddled into the crook of his father's arm and yawned. Both men grinned. A meeting of eyes showed that each remembered his own childhood in that moment. A sweet interlude on a wild night.

Onie spoke in a low voice. As he added a singsong note to it, he watched to see if Frank drifted into sleep. "What about the man staying in your livery?"

One brow lifted. The ice blue eyes widened. "How'd you learn 'bout Smith? Jah, I have let him stay."

Onie's eyes narrowed. "Never known you to do that before. Why'd you let him?"

Large shoulders shrugged carefully so as not to upset the groggy boy. "Just out of the army. I served. He served. It seemed the right thing to do."

That piece of news fit into Onie's theory. "So, did you see him arrive with a gun? Maybe one he kept after leaving the army?"

The wavy blonde head nodded. "Jah, one of those new guns. He crowed the day he showed me. 'An 1868 Springfield,' Smith said. Then he showed me the bullet."

Shoving two fingers into his vest pocket, Onie pulled out the slug. "Look anything like that?"

A shadow fell over his brother-in-law's features. With a dark frown, he carefully leaned forward without waking his sleeping son. "The same, 50 calibers. Smith, he shot at your woman?"

Returning the bullet to his pocket, Onie slipped into his sheriff's role. "Have you seen the man tonight?"

"His horse and gear disappeared from the livery. Not even a 'thank you' for the place to stay." Ezra's face showed regret and sadness rather than anger at Smith's behavior. Ruby married a good man.

"How about when you talked to Smith? He say where he was headed or why he came to Bailey's Meadow?"

Ezra laid Frank on the sofa beside him and covered the boy with a nearby afghan. "He was drifting home eastward. Told me he had the chance at a job in town so he stopped."

The large man snorted and continued. "Some job, but I don't pry. Like others here, we let people leave their past behind when they come west."

"Nothing else?"

At the other's coaxing tone, Ezra rubbed his chin thoughtfully. "He did say the job was for Mr. B."

Lifting and lowering his shoulders slightly, he explained. "I thought he meant Bailey."

"Ever hear him mention Blakenship or Arnold's Corner?"

Interest lit light blue eyes. "Arnold's Corner? In Massachusetts? Jah, said that was his hometown."

More pieces fit together for Onie. Blakenship and this Smith easily could be connected. The telegram to Smith came from that town and was signed with a *B*. That matched what Ezra said.

Was it a coincidence that a man from Sookie's hometown owned a rifle that fired 50 caliber slugs and happened to be in Bailey's Meadow when someone shot at her? He refused to believe in coincidences. That Occam's razor principle again. The simplest answer was correct.

With prodding, Ezra described Smith, physically as well as his personality and any small motions he did repeatedly. Seems the man had a nervous habit of touching a thumb to his nose. That might help identify him when Onie arrived at Crawford's saloon.

Now outside the saloon's backdoor, Onie stiffened his shoulders and checked his gun. He made sure to stop by the warehouse before heading here. He knew fresh percussion caps guaranteed the gun would not misfire if he needed to defend himself against Smith.

A knock on the backdoor drew someone's attention. He heard soft steps on the other side of the poorly made door. It opened crookedly and Crawford's wife scowled at him.

"Whatcha want, sheriff?" She bit out the title with scorn. The wife had a bad history with lawmen, he guessed.

"Looking for the man who shot my wife. Want to take a peek from your backroom."

Some of the hardness left her mouth. "Yeah, I heard 'bout that." Moving back, she waved him into the room.

Not saying anything else, she disappeared into the tavern's main room carrying a plate of sandwiches. Onie heard they served a limited menu here. Even when he burned their supper, he never considered bringing Letty to Crawford's for something to eat.

His stomach twisted at the mere thought of exposing his baby girl to this kind of life. Must be some of Ruby's teaching about godly living stayed with him. His choices after leaving home were about as opposite of her teaching as could be. Funny that so much came back to him once he parented a child.

Last evening, Wren spoke about Christ as if he provided their way to Bailey's Meadow instead of the hard-earned money that Onie sent to the matchmaker. At the time, it irked him. Now, he thought over it.

Some force tugged at his mind, urging him to consider the conversation again. Occam's razor. The simplest answer would be that the Lord led Mrs. Crenshaw to the sisters when they most needed her and when she had the perfect groom for Sookie to marry.

And he and Sookie did fit together like a hand and glove. He felt that at the train station in Plattsmouth. Who better to marry a woman who communicated by sign than someone who had experience with sign language?

As a child he believed in God and His power in people's lives. Wild living and then Alicia's death hardened his heart. Something about Sookie's arrival softened it again. It created a strange urging in him that maybe God cared enough to want Onyx Hastings back.

For the first time since Alicia breathed her last, Onie whispered a brief prayer. It bit into his pride to admit he needed anyone's help. Still, he followed the sensation deep inside him.

"Please, help me find Smith."

Peace miraculously pushed out the dread and anger that gripped him since Sookie's injury. Clear-headed and determined, he peered through the barely opened door. One man after another looked familiar, men he knew and dismissed. Then opening the door a few inches more, he spied a short man wearing a weathered army uniform.

Watching him, Onie swallowed a laugh of triumph when the man repeatedly thumbed his nose while speaking with Bailey's oldest boy. Not a boy any longer, really, and he wanted to prove it by hanging out at the saloon. The mayor moaned only yesterday to Onie about that.

He stopped to consider how best to corner the man. From where Smith stood at the long bar, Onie knew he would need to go exit and re-enter by the main door. If only someone would come along before he went into the tavern. He figured then he would look like one of the many farmers or townsmen wanting to spend time with a friend.

A second prayer in one evening whispered across his lips. Another assault on his godless pride. If he had faced this situation yesterday, Onie would have confidently burst into the saloon, believing no one could get the better of him. That pride popped like a soap bubble tonight and he saw how much he needed what only God could provide.

"Lord, you can send someone to go in there with me. I'm believing it."

As he left the backroom and stepped out into the inky night, Onie snorted derisively. Who asked the Lord to send someone into a tavern? It made no sense to ask God to make someone behave in a sinful manner. No, that was one prayer the Lord would ignore.

Even as he thought that, Onie rounded the corner of the building and saw a shadow approaching the front door. They met under the lantern hung by the entrance. Recognizing the man, Onie wanted to laugh aloud at the result of his prayer. Before he even whispered it, the Lord moved this man into position to help Onie.

Wiley Schwartz stared at him oddly, holding a telegram in his right hand. "Somethin' wrong, Hastings? Maybe you're here lookin' for the same man I am?"

Onie pressed his lips together and tapped a finger to his chin a few times to consider that. "Smith getting another wire from the mysterious *B*?"

Wiley shushed him with a finger to his lips. "Now, I can't go tellin' other people's business to everyone and his Aunt Tilly." While he spoke, the man winked and nodded at Onie.

The sheriff explained his plan to reach Smith. Wiley cast a nervous glance at Onie's Colt Peacemaker. Nevertheless, he nodded and entered alongside the sheriff as if they came together. He shook his head just once at the sheriff's muttering about God providing Wiley as a cover. Strange to hear that proud man give God credit for anything.

Immediately, Wiley headed to Smith. After all, he'd given the man a telegram before and recognized him. With a relaxed grin, Onie walked beside him.

Out the corner of his mouth, the sheriff hissed, "Smile, Schwartz."

With an effort the other man worked at it. He imagined sitting at a table and gossiping. That tipped his lips upward into a wide grin.

At a call from Schwartz, Smith whirled on the telegrapher. He moved for his gun's long barrel, only relaxing when he glimpsed Wiley with the telegram in hand. Leaning casually against the bar, Smith sneered at the small man.

"Nearly blew a hole in you, old man. Don't sneak up on a soldier!"

"Quite a piece you got here," Wiley cackled. "Get that from the army?"

The man nodded and Wiley pressed forward with Onie's plan. "Never seen one. Mind if I take a look."

Smith eyed him suspiciously and looked at Onie who had joined him on his right side, also leaning against the bar. At that man's wide, welcoming smile, Smith relaxed and handed the gun out, barrel first.

"Careful! It's loaded."

As Smith lowered his arm, a hand grasped it and something snapped onto his wrist. With a twist, his other wrist fit into the shackle easily. Unable to turn because of a strong grip pinching his neck, he looked over his shoulder and saw the same wide smile on the man who entered Crawford's with the telegrapher.

"What's the big idea?"

He roared his words like a lion. Onie considered him, one eyebrow arched. Smith looked more like a sly fox caught in a trap rather than king of the jungle.

"We're headed to my jail so you can answer some questions. I 'specially want to hear about Blakenship."

The mention of that man's name caused a sudden whiteness around Smith's mouth. Onie watched him carefully for a reaction. That change in the man pleased him. One more piece to prove his theory.

Shoving a hand into the middle of Smith's back, the sheriff pushed him out of the silent saloon. A mixture of frowns and questions of, "Did he shoot your woman?" followed them. Onie kept his smile in place and his attention fixed on the prisoner.

In the dark, he spoke. "Stop a minute. Which is your horse?"

Stony silence met his query. A pinch to the man's neck earned the sheriff a vile oath before Smith lifted cuffed hands to point at a pie bald tied at a hitching post near the edge of the lantern light. Onie called out an order to Wiley who had followed them out of the saloon, once again holding the telegram Smith dropped.

"Get the horse and bring it to my warehouse. I want to look through his things."

A growl of anger had Smith struggling to free his neck from Onie's grip. "You got no right."

Onie grabbed the man's arm, resisting the urge to shake him. "You shooting at my wife gives me the right."

Smith stiffened, falling silent. "Nothing to say about that? Don't want to brag to me about your trapdoor rifle like you did with Ezra Kline?"

Under his hand, Onie felt the fight leave the man. Instead, a trembling energy replaced it, like a rabbit caught in a snare. That was one more piece that reinforced Onie's theory.

Forcing the man to start walking again, the clip clop of the horse followed behind them. Wiley muttered words Onie ignored. His sole focus remained on Smith.

"Might as well start talking. What's your real name?"

At the prisoner's silent refusal, the sheriff chuckled. "Don't worry. I'm like as not to find your army papers in that saddlebag I saw on your horse."

Onie heard a soft groan sound from the criminal. He pushed him further. "And I bet I'll find a letter or two from Blankenship about this plan."

This time the man's groan echoed in the still night. "No small-town sheriff shoulda been able to sniff out a man's scheme."

"Could be you and Blakenship forgot to consider where my help's coming from."

Oddly, suddenly, a verse Ruby taught him years ago flitted into Onie's mind. "Don't you know Psalm one hundred and twenty-one?"

The prisoner hooted. "The bible? Who cares?"

Onie worked to mute any hints of pride in his voice. This was not about him. "Well, it tells you how I figured out what you and the man in Arnold's Corner are about."

Scorn dripped from the question. "How's that?"

"You see, that verse says where I get my help."

He paused with the man outside the warehouse. As much as he hated bringing a criminal this close to his family, the building housed the only jail cell. With ringing sincerity, Onie breathed out words that reconnected him with the savior he left behind in his youth.

"My help comes from the Lord."

CHAPTER 7

Through the darkness preceding dawn, Sheriff Onie Hastings trudged wearily to the rooms at the back of his warehouse. Both the facts Homer Earl had admitted—Smith's real name—and the contents of the telegram weighed heavily on his slumped shoulders.

Earlier he believed tracking down and arresting the gunman would keep Sookie safe. He no longer felt sure of that. Reading the latest telegram left him in no doubt of further danger.

Four simple words. On way. Close now.

He needed a description of Blakenship from either his wife or Wren. That way he more easily would spot the man when he arrived. Having a train stop outside the town and the help of a deputy would make things a heap simpler. Still, Onie knew he could count on Bailey's older boys to keep their eyes on whichever direction he asked each to watch. That would have to do.

A story from Greek mythology flitted into his head. It fit this situation perfectly. He lopped off one head, true. But arresting Earl did little while the hydra still lived. And that hydra in the form of Blakenship posed the greatest danger.

Shaking his head to clear it of silly comparisons, Onie dismissed the Greek myth from his thoughts. He expected a flesh and blood person by the name of Blakenship to arrive soon and not a monster. At least, he believed the man would come.

Focusing on the dark path in front of him, Onie halted. Movement twitched ahead and to his right. There, in the concealing clump of elms, a body shifted. He would bet his business on it being a person, not that he was a betting man.

Easing closer to the walls of the warehouse, he blended into the extra darkness cast by its shadow. Backing up, he rounded the building's edge and stopped. The layout of his backyard with its clump of trees ran through his mind like a map before he hastily formed a plan.

Stepping softly, lightly, to avoid breaking fallen twigs, he moved behind the trees. Gun drawn, Onie glimpsed the movement again, this time close in front of him as he walked into the small clump. Close by finally, he cocked the Colt and held his breath.

Stiffening, the shadow quickly raised his arms. "I'm not carrying money. No use robbing me. Or shooting me for that matter."

In the silent night, Onie recognized that voice. He spoke to the man earlier at the school meeting. Reynolds Harper!

"Doggone it, I almost shot you, Harper! What you doing on my property?" The anxiety and cold determination of minutes before erupted as anger in the sheriff's voice.

"I'm watching, of course. With you busy, someone needed to be sure Miss Donaldson came to no harm."

Harper's proper speech sounded odd in Onie's ears. He so seldom heard the stiff tones of his youth. Few people possessed that level of education and social status in the farmlands of Nebraska.

The older man's growl split the quiet. "She's Mrs. Hastings, not Miss Donaldson. And I don't think I like your attentions to my wife." As he spoke, Onie holstered his pistol.

Harper bent to touch something. In the dark, the rasp of a match on metal sounded. Sudden light flared from the lantern the taller man held to look at the sheriff.

"I, uh, I mean, uh, Miss Donaldson. She will be my wife one day."

Onie laughed loudly enough to bring a cry from inside the rooms where his family slept. Looking that way, he saw a candle flare to life in Letty's bedroom. When he challenged Harper, Onie did so in a whisper.

"You crazy? Wren's only seventeen and you don't even know her."

"I'm twenty-nine. Old enough to know my mind, and I've claimed a nice section of land. Soon, I'll build her a real house and then come for her."

Confidence rang in his voice. "I know we're meant to be together."

Great. Now he had to deal with a stalker along as well as a dangerous man intent on killing his wife. This night was one for the books.

"Go home, Harper. Don't come here unless someone invites you. You hear me?"

Wide shoulders slumped as the other man nodded. He turned, carrying his lantern and walked toward Ezra's livery stable. Knowing the man held a lighted lantern, Onie grimaced inwardly.

"And don't burn down the livery with that." Onie added the last command in a tone that said he was sure the stable would be reduced to smoldering cinders by morning.

A door opened. A figure with long hair floating around her stood in the doorway, holding high a candle. "Who's there?"

His sister-in-law's voice trembled as she hissed her question. Onie wanted to growl his frustration. How could he keep the women safe? Wren lacked the common sense to stay inside.

Fatigue swamped his body while he breathed out a soft petition for help. God alone had the answers. Onie felt too tired to worry over the future.

"Get inside, girl! No telling if someone'll come after you this time. Even if I do have the shooter in a cell."

A loud sigh of relief sent the candlelight flickering. She stepped backward and he followed her inside. "Your sister okay?"

By the yellow glow, he watched Wren's lips curve upward. "Yes, and I am glad to hear the caring in your voice. She deserves a man who'll protect her."

"Don't get mushy on me."

Embarrassment and exhaustion brought a denial to Onie's lips. "I take care of everyone under my roof."

She hummed. "You didn't ask about Letty, just your wife."

"Well, she's just what you said—my wife." Softly, he added, "And I want years with her, not merely days."

Grinning, the girl twirled and headed to the bedroom she shared with the baby. At the doorway, she stopped. "Who was out there with you?"

A snort told her how he felt as he muttered, "Your admirer. Thinks you're gonna marry him."

Her gasp did put out the candle this time. "What!"

She hissed the word and waited for Onie to explain. He shrugged his shoulders as he passed her. Not saying anymore, he twisted the knob and entered the room he shared with Sookie.

He removed his clothes and lifted the blankets, hoping not to wake her. Focused on moving carefully so as not to rock the mattress, the hand that touched him in the dark made him jump.

Sookie's fingers found his palm and then threaded through his, squeezing once before she sighed and slipped back into sleep. He leaned over her to kiss her gently, the kind of kiss that reaffirmed their marriage. No passion, just an intimacy that came from knowing he and she were free to touch one another.

Laying down beside his wife, Onie worked to dismiss the day's troubles from his mind. For the first time since going off to college, he said a prayer. Peacefully, sleep overtook him.

St. Joseph, Missouri

He laid awake, unable to sleep. Usually, he fell asleep easily. Silas Blakenship chalked that up to living a clean life and having a clear conscience.

Tonight, he struggled to keep his eyes closed. As he drifted into sleep, Sookie Donaldson's face floated before his eyes. An hour or so earlier, he slipped into sleep and woke from a nightmare. In the dream, that woman held the key before his eyes while dancing on her parents' graves—graves he still might need to open.

The plan seemed perfect. He had what he wanted—almost. And, the night before, he visited a saloon where he joined a poker game. The five hundred dollars he won rested in his wallet.

For the time being, his hunger for the tables stopped gripping him. He could concentrate on making the little bird sing for him. He needed that key.

O'Connor sent men after him before Silas left for Nebraska. No dirty child with a note that time but actual thugs. He did his best to use small words and explain to the muscled idiots why he needed a key to retrieve the deed locked away in a bank. Even days later he remembered their dark stares. One had growled and made a threatening gesture while the other grabbed Silas's arm to twist it painfully behind his back.

Silas never suffered pain well. That encouraged him to telegraph Earl and order Sookie's murder. He needed Wren to be helpless and welcoming when he miraculously arrived.

Like all of his plans, he expected this one to be perfect. His other plan worked beautifully, at least it did until he ran into the stone wall of the lockbox. Frustration bubbled up as he thought of the smug banker, Robert Grant. Unable to stop it, Silas shrieked out his angry resentment.

On the other side of the hotel wall, someone slammed a fist. "Shut up in there!"

He owned a handgun. The man's bellow sent Silas reaching for it. Caution somehow curbed his impulse. That ill-mannered man would not side-track him from his new, perfect plan.

Silas would save all his irritation and anger for Wren Donaldson.

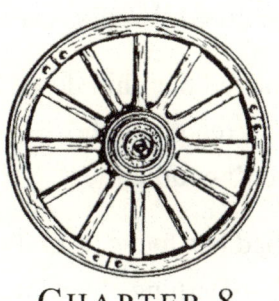

CHAPTER 8

Letty's chubby hand chased the bubbles while Wren bathed her in the white enameled dishpan. The pan sat in the dry sink below the kitchen window. Sunbeams streamed in, making the baby's hair glisten gold in the light.

Sookie, sitting in a kitchen chair, silently laughed along with the baby's sweet giggles. After two days in bed, she refused to let the headache keep her there any longer. She was a new wife and needed to see about her home and family.

Stomping her foot once, Sookie waited for Wren to look her way. It was their signal, a little like calling her sister's name to grab her attention. When her sister looked away from the baby, Sookie held out her arms.

"Are you sure you can manage her? Letty's heavy." Doubt colored Wren's words.

Her sister moved her chin down twice and pursed her lips. Wren knew those lips well. That sign meant, "Don't coddle me."

Wren returned her focus to Letty. She washed the baby's hair, something she waited to do until Letty's fun in the water came to an end. Placing a towel over her shoulder, Wren lifted the wailing little one and wrapped her in the linen. Finally, she placed her in Sookie's lap to let her sister finish drying her.

Mother and daughter stared at each other as Letty stopped crying. Sookie made kissing motions with her lips. One chubby hand reached up. The fingers touched her new mother's mouth. Under those fingers, Sookie made the exaggerated pucker again. Giggles pealed from the girl's own rosebud lips.

At that moment, Onie walked into the house. The sight stayed his steps. Two beautiful faces close together, made more lovely by their shared joy. Troubles and danger outside this kitchen ceased for a time as he allowed the sight to fill his heart.

Both females looked his way and the scene ceased. He entered the room and made his way to where Sookie sat. With one finger, he gently stroked Letty's cheek before he leaned down to kiss Sookie. That kiss was quick and possessive.

Darting a look at her sister who presented her back to them, Sookie tapped his chest. He laughed. "Yes, I'm all yours, Sweetheart."

The glow in his eyes told his wife what she needed to know. Her husband enjoyed her possessiveness. The brush of his lips on hers certainly assured her that he shared this possessive feeling. Faithfulness and protectiveness ranked high on her mental list of what made a man attractive. Onyx Hastings not only looked great, but the person inside drew her as no other man could or ever would.

Taking one hand from the baby's back, she flapped it out with the palm up. *What's happening?*

He ignored her, tickling the towel-wrapped baby. She poked his chest. At his shocked look, she repeated her sign.

"Wren, come take the baby, please." He called to his sister-in-law, knowing her willingness to help. She and her sister tenderly adored the girl, something he thanked God for silently as the young woman lifted Letty from his wife's lap.

Lowering his voice, he filled in details of the shooter and those brief words in the telegram. "I've been sending wires to Mrs. Crenshaw. Your cousin's concerned, especially since her detective discovered a few interesting facts about the accident."

While he whispered that word, Onie touched the scar on her throat. His wife reached up to remove his hand. He allowed her to take his fingers away. He replaced those fingers with his mouth, kissing the spot soothingly.

"It's part of you. I think all of you is precious and lovely because it shows the strong woman I am coming to know." Sincerity gleamed from his eyes and Sookie nodded. She had no reason to doubt what he said.

She gave him a questioning look and motioned a sign that was new to him. Frustrated, she repeated it. He only raised his hands and shook his head.

"Sorry. I guess I don't know that one." Saying that, he called for Wren.

She walked into the kitchen holding a freshly clothed Letty. "What do you need?"

Sookie stomped her foot once and rapidly signed. At her sister's nod, she relaxed slightly. Onie realized once this trouble passed that he would need to memorize his wife's dictionary.

"My sister wants you to tell her what our cousin wrote in her telegrams." Wren arched a finely shaped eyebrow. "I'd like to hear that too."

Moving to lean against the dry sink, Onie folded his arms across his broad chest and looked from one woman to the other. "The accident wasn't one."

At their blank looks, he explained. "I mean, the police declared it was murder as some unknown person tampered with the carriage."

Wren moved swiftly. She stopped by Sookie's chair and gripped her sister's hand, the need for comfort clear on her young face. The girl might be nearly eighteen. Even so, she needed her older sister's mothering and protection. Needed his protection too, for that matter.

Sookie made a tumbling motion with one hand. He recognized that sign. She wanted him to get on with his retelling.

"According to the detective, he asked a handwriting expert to examine your father's will filed at the county courthouse during probate. The signature definitely proved false. In fact, a judge issued a warrant for Silas Blakenship's arrest only yesterday."

His wife rubbed her right hand down her left forearm. *How?*

"How will he be caught? I don't know."

Unfolding his arms, Onie ran one hand down his face. "I wired the US marshal in St. Joe, Missouri. Thought he might come up or send another man already in Nebraska."

She poked his chest tenderly, dark eyes burning into his. He shook his head. "I think this might be beyond me."

He ran fingers through his hair in a frustrated gesture. "Nonetheless, that doesn't mean Bailey's older boys and I won't try to stop the man."

Two fingers raised in the air. Sookie pointed over her right shoulder afterward and pointed at his chest again. He shook his head. "Those two men yesterday. I simply chased them out of town after you told me their plan."

Sookie stood outside the mercantile along with the oldest Bailey boy, Kip. They waited for Wren to finish purchasing something she refused to buy in front of him. He refused to leave Sookie alone in the store.

"Sheriff's sure you're the target, ma'am," Kip argued.

That meant she stood on the newly built boardwalk in front of Mr. Bailey's store. When Wren took too long, Kip ducked back into the store to complain.

"I'll be able to see you through the window, Mrs. Hastings. And, I'll leave the door open to be able to get to you fast." He told her getting her home was a "priority" and Sookie knew he was echoing a word he's heard from her husband.

Once she stood alone, the mute woman pushed her body against the building's exterior wall. The white boards gleamed in the sunshine, so the building lent no concealing shadow. Nevertheless, it gave her a feeling of safety.

Two men stood at the edge of the same building, huddled together in conversation. As they spoke, their words gradually grew louder as their hand gestures flew. No wonder she noticed them.

As the two yelled, Sookie caught some of the words. "Bank. Grab. Money." Though the words came separately, she easily put the scheme together.

One man noticed her staring their way. He pulled his companion by the jacket toward her. The man pulled back, pushing in his heels to pause.

"She's listening. What we gonna do?" The one who noticed her hissed those words loudly enough so that she easily heard them.

The other man snorted a dismissal. "Nah. She can't hear. Saw her using those funny hand gestures to talk."

Closer to her now, they continued planning how to rob the new bank. She looked away, splitting her attention between the window and the door to get Kip's attention. Finally, he stopped watching her sister and looked toward Sookie.

She interlaced her fingers and turned them up. Kip turned to Wren and then pointed at the window. Sookie watched Wren speak and Kip race to the door. He burst out onto the boardwalk, frightening the two would-be robbers.

As the schemers raced away, Kip's charge slipped her wedding band up and down in agitation. Kip stared, shaking his head. "I don't get it, Mrs. Hastings."

"She wants her husband." Wren finally emerged from the store, clutching a soft package wrapped in brown paper.

After that, she told Onie about the two men. He and the banker chased them out of town, each holding a shotgun aimed at them. Since they only planned and did not commit the crime, he saw no way or need to arrest the two.

In the present, she considered his belief about Blakenship being more than he could handle. Both palms went up as she shrugged. Quickly, those palms came together in front of Sookie's chest, and her chin raised to look toward the rough boards forming their ceiling. She peeked at him through one closed eye as she bowed her head and felt him reach for her hands.

"Dear Father, how we need your help. I know right along you've been protecting Sookie and Wren. Thank you. But I need wisdom and strength to be your hands and feet."

He waited for her to add to the prayer. She spoke so clearly to him with her eyes and gestures he forgot she could not truly speak aloud.

"I ask for this in the name of Jesus."

Toneless lips moved. He watched her continue to pray. When she opened her eyes to return his gaze, she smiled.

Putting a finger to his chest, she removed it and made her sign for prayer. Her features scrunched into a question as she did this. Somehow, she must have sensed his distance from the Lord on the day they married. That had to be why she asked.

"Ruby's tried to get me back into church. Something changed after you were shot." Onie rubbed a hand over the back of his neck, thinking. His wife stared intently, waiting.

"I, well, felt an urge. Sort of a hunger, I guess, to pray as I looked for the man who shot you. Like a silent voice telling me to trust that the Lord would take me back. Actually, that God wanted to hear from me."

Onie expected humor or disbelief on Sookie's face. None of that appeared on her cupid bow lips. She only bobbed her head as those lips and the corners of her eyes both tipped slightly upward.

Pleasure. Understanding. She conveyed all that with only a brief change in her features.

"After that, I told the Lord what I needed to happen. Kind of like laying out a fleece. What that man in the bible did. Gideon, I think." She tipped her head up and down in a small movement to confirm that he had the correct name.

"Time and again last night, God provided. Actually guided what I did." He paused. "You don't think that's odd?"

Grasping his larger hands in hers, Sookie's closed mouth spread in a wide grin. She hugged his hands to her chest and shook back and forth. Onie's mind struggled to remember before the sign's meaning came to him.

147

I'm so happy. "I'm glad too. We can both trust the Lord in this situation."

Onie's face clouded. "I am confused about one thing." Sookie dropped his hands, otherwise unmoving as she listened closely.

"Why hasn't Blakenship already arrived? The telegram made me think he planned to be in Bailey's Meadow the day after he sent it."

Squeezing his eyes shut, Onie pinched the bridge of his nose. The start of a headache gnawed at him.

Moving behind him, his wife's hands kneaded tight muscles. Groaning in pleasure, he tipped his head toward his chest. "Haven't had anyone do that since I was a kid. Feels good." Another groan left his lips.

"Should we come in there? Sounds a little, well—" Wren peeked into the kitchen, breaking off what she tried to say. Her features showed confusion. She had nothing to compare those sounds with even though they embarrassed her.

Lifting his head, her brother-in-law threw her a wolfish grin. "Come in only if you can stand the sight of a woman massaging her husband's neck."

"If that's all it is." Wren carried the baby to her father and plopped the heavy child into his lap.

Immediately, Letty patted his cheeks and babbled. He spent so much time away from her, but even so she reached for him whenever they shared a moment. Their bond humbled him and at the same time filled him with an incredible joy.

"Time for me to make supper. Also, someone kept babbling, 'Dada' and tried to escape the parlor." Letty's babble seemed to agree with her aunt.

The younger woman laughed at the girl. She busily stirred up the coals in the small stove ahead of moving a black iron skillet to the burner.

"Ham and eggs okay for supper? Something easy and quick."

Sookie's hands flew, and her sister shook her head. "I'm happy to do it. You finish caring for your husband."

149

Fingers rubbed and bit into knotted muscles. Both his females focused their whole attention on him and Onie soaked in the moment. He was a blessed man.

He must be cursed! Silas slunk out of the hotel room by the stairs attached to the end of each floor. The rickety stairs lay against the building, meant only as an escape in case of fire.

In the early hours before dawn, Silas used them for escape. The only fire burned inside him from the terrible sense of being pursued.

He meant to move on days ago. The poker tables called to him. They were Sirens pulling him toward the rocks. Well, he'd hit the rocks last night when a slick gambler joined the table where Silas sat with a pile of winnings.

If only he could figure out how the man cheated him. Got every cent he brought with him. Even took Silas's gold watch.

The man had to be a cheat. Silas won prior to the man joining the game. No way would he have lost otherwise.

So he slunk away in the darkness before a new day broke. He had nothing left over for the bill. With no choice, he sneaked off like a common thief.

No money for a train ticket either. He should have wired The Emporium for funds. That might have worked if Shasta still worked there. Silas hadn't found the time to replace his clerk.

He could have sent a wire to Robert Grant for money. Still would, but in a different town. The other part what cursed him made it imperative to leave St. Joseph immediately.

At the poker table the night before, one of the men mentioned a US marshal. Supposedly, the lawman asked about a man matching Silas's description. Even said Silas's name.

"Heard you're a murderer. That true?" Every eye at the table pinned him like a bug.

Silas could only shake his head vehemently. Getting rid of impediments to a plan wasn't the same as murder. He didn't try to explain that to the idiots who stared at him.

At that moment, the gambler joined them. His brocade vest and fine suit should have warned Silas.

This man worked the tables for a living. Silas would have left if that accusation minutes before had not muddied his mind.

The curse! It started earlier, when he knew he needed the key. Nothing worked out with his plan since that moment. The whole world came against him now!

Biting back tears, Silas gripped his carpetbag's handle and stiffened his shoulders. A sudden wind pulled at his whiskers. It reminded him that he needed to reglue them. Planning his escape from the hotel occupied his mind earlier, and he forgot to do that.

Pressing them against his smooth skin, he hoped the pressure would be enough to keep the fringe of hair in place. In a shadow outside the livery, Silas set down his carpetbag and waited. No sounds hinted at anyone sleeping inside.

Finally, something was going his way. That thought buoyed him as he slipped in and grabbed the necessary tack. He would need it and someone's saddle to keep his plan going. Nothing was a crime if it helped him realize his plan.

Horses stood in the shadow of the building. Silas easily entered the coral and separated a mare from the group. She snorted in surprise but allowed him to slip the bridle over her head. He struggled to lift the saddle, and finally led the horse out of the enclosure to stop it by the fence.

He tied his bag to the saddle and climbed the fence's boards to mount. In the saddle, Silas smiled and let loose a high-pitched giggle. He'd done it.

A shout rose from the house behind the livery. Using a small whip, the pudgy shadow slapped the sides of the mare as he drove cruel heels into her. Fright set the animal racing from her home.

A blast from a shotgun sounded. Not feeling anything, Silas giggled at knowing the man missed hitting him. Still, fear drove him to whip the horse harder. No common laborer would impede his plan.

He had a bird to snatch. A key to find. A crime boss expecting payment. Once that was done, Silas could return to the gambling tables at the Pleasure Palace.

The hunger would be assuaged. And the curse? The death of both sisters would see an end to that.

CHAPTER 9

"He's back. This is the fourth night. Doesn't that man ever sleep at his own place?"

Wren let the flour sack curtain slip into place again as she turned away from the window. Hands on her hips and a mulish look on her face clearly conveyed her opinion of Reynolds Harper.

If Sookie had any doubt, Wren confirmed how her sister felt by stomping to the door and opening it. "Reynolds Harper, go home!"

He stepped out of the shadowy elms. "You're my girl. I plan to keep you safe.

"I'm no one's girl." She yelled the words.

Taking a deep breath and letting it out slowly, Wren reasoned with the man. "I'm my own woman.

I have a brother-in-law and the Bailey boys to protect me."

Standing with legs apart—a warrior stance—Reynolds hissed his reply. "I will not let that oldest Bailey boy get a jump on wooing you."

Wren threw her hands up. "Fine. Stay there."

Her tone softened in the next moment. "Only, come in and get a cup of hot coffee before Sister and I go to bed."

Behind her, the aforementioned sister raised her brows. She stomped her foot and Wren turned. *Why?*

At her sister's sign, Wren shrugged. "He means well. A little Christian charity seems, uh, due him."

The young man crossed the threshold and shut the door behind him. "Thank you, honey."

Wren stiffened at the word. The playful grin he wore brought a smile to Sookie's face. Her sister glowered, unmoved by his expression.

"Tonight's not cold as the last one, but I won't turn down an offer for coffee."

Sookie walked fingers across her palm and shrugged. Reynolds watched the older sister and then turned to Wren. "Will you translate, please?"

Not speaking, Wren set a tin cup filled with dark liquid in front of the man. She reached around him to shove the small cream pitcher and sugar bowl closer to him. At a stomp from her sister, the young woman looked her way and frowned.

After rapid gestures, Wren sat. Focusing her gaze on her sister and not the lanky man, she answered his question. "My sister wants you to tell her where you're from?"

"Only from the East, ma'am. That seems enough explanation for people in this area." He fixed his coffee, pouring a dab of cream and ignoring the sugar.

More rapid hand gestures. Sighing, Wren obeyed her sister and worked to start a conversation with this visitor, meeting his gaze. "What are you planning to grow on your land?"

Lowering the cup from lips he patted with a white linen handkerchief, Harper smiled politely. Something in that quirk of his mouth drew her.

Looking at him for the first time in light rather than the usual shadows, Wren noticed with surprise he was not as young as she had thought. The man seemed to be almost Onie's age, around thirty or more. Not a calf-eyed youth.

His voice pulled her out of her thoughts. "Wheat seems to be the crop of choice here on the plains. I already have a few chickens and a cow. Perhaps a milk herd would be a good source of income." He stared intently at Wren as he spoke.

She colored under his unbreaking scrutiny. "Why are you so fixed on me? You don't know me. We haven't even gone for a walk together and already you plan for us to marry?"

Reynolds Harper broke the stare. Fidgeting he moved his gaze to his nearly empty coffee cup. "I get, uhm, insights."

"What do you mean?" Wren's eyes narrowed and one brow arched in question.

"I got one about coming west. I knew I'd find the woman to marry and a job that satisfied my restlessness."

"And have you found that job?"

"Very close. Something about the land I claimed called to me. Breaking the soil, removing rocks. Each physical task assures me that I'm where I need to be."

The sisters exchanged blank glances. He smiled a boyish grin and shrugged. "You don't understand that at all, do you?"

"No." Wren's emphatic response was meant to discourage him.

Again, Reynolds shrugged wide shoulders. "You don't need to know. So many other things require our attention."

He rose, "And speaking of that, I must return to my lookout spot."

Sookie gestured. Wren caught the movement from the corner of her eye and concentrated as her sister repeated the signs. "Sookie would like you to come for supper tomorrow before you watch the house."

Reynolds smiled at the woman. "Thank you. I gladly accept your invitation." Bowing slightly at the waist, he left.

A frightened cry lifted the hairs on Sookie's neck. She rose, ready to race to Letty. Wren stopped her with a hand on her sister's arm.

"You need rest. I, well, need time. I'll just sit up and think while I rock her."

They walked together. At the bedroom door, Sookie cast a worried look from the closed door to her sister. "It's fine. Rest."

Onie's second Colt Peacemaker lay in a drawer on his side of the bed. Sitting on the still-made bed, Sookie drew it out. Yesterday, he showed her the steps so she could fire it. Repeating them mentally, she readied the gun.

At a single, muffled scream from the room next to her, Sookie moved to the window. Throwing up the sash, she angled the gun and shot upward, calculating an area where the bullet could harmlessly return to the ground. Help would come.

The door flew open with a bang. Sookie turned and saw it rebound off the wall. Even with darkness filling the room, she clearly made out the shape of a gun. The large shape waved a revolver wildly from corner to corner of the room.

"Hello, Sookie. Why aren't you dead?"

"I came from St. Louis as soon as I got the other detective's telegram. Bad business, as I understand it."

Max Bryant, a Pinkerton, surprised Onie by arriving late in the day. He and the Baileys watched the stranger ride in, expecting to see a marshal's badge. When the man showed a Pinkerton shield-shaped badge instead, the sheriff's disappointment showed clearly.

"Not the welcome I expected." Bryant's rueful chuckle gently rebuked Onie's lack of manners.

"I'm sorry, Bryant. We'd been hoping a US marshal would come, what with the warrant for Blakenship and all."

"Well, that one's an interesting character. My boss wanted someone to help you with him."

The man refused the chair Onie offered and stood in front of the wide desk. They were in the office section of the warehouse, not far from the one cell that was the town's only jail. Earl lay sleeping on the cot inside of it.

Onie leaned against the edge of the simple pine desk and waited, a desk he built himself and it showed in the piece's crude lines. When nothing more was said, he prodded the man. "So, what is so different that a Pinkerton agent needs to travel here?"

Bryant cleared his throat, taking a sip of the strong coffee from a tin cup. "Silas Blakenship died ten years ago. His twin disappeared about the same time."

Bryant looked meaningfully at the sheriff. "The neighbors figured the twin poisoned him."

"A history of murder. Fits with Blakenship for sure."

Straightening from the edge of the desk, Onie pointed a finger as if ready to say more. The bang of his warehouse door halted him. Kip Bailey raced across the open space of the building.

"Man's at the livery. Fits the description." Kip leaned forward with his hands on his thighs, gasping for breath.

Bryant immediately picked up the rifle he brought with him. "Good job, son." Eyeing the sheriff, Bryant allowed one side of his mouth to lift in a mock grin. "You ready for the big time?"

Masking any emotion, Onie shrugged his shoulders. He drew the Colt from its holster and led Bryant out of the warehouse. Kip made to follow, but Onie held up a hand.

"You stay out of it now. Your job's done." The words pulled a disappointed frown from the young man. Nevertheless, he stayed put.

The two men crept through the shadows cast by store buildings on the main street of Bailey's Meadow. Ezra's livery sat at the end of those buildings, on the other side of town from Onie's warehouse and one street over. Reaching it, they eased around the side toward the open door where light spilled out and met the darkness.

With his rifle held in front of him, Bryant jumped quickly into the livery. Onie hung back, waiting for the wanted man to try an escape. An irritated voice called for him.

"Onie, get in here and tell this man who I am!" Ezra sounded irate but not afraid. That big man faced danger before. Obviously the Pinkerton's rifle failed to frighten him.

"Come on out, Bryant. That's my brother-in-law."

The detective left the livery, followed by a frowning Ezra. "Found the beaten animal tied in there, worse for wear. I don't know where the owner went." He growled those words and went back inside.

Bryant lowered his rifle and rubbed his thumb and two fingers on his forehead. "We don't know what all Earl wired Blakenship about your wife. Maybe he knows where to find her."

Not speaking, Onie whirled and ran toward his end of town. This time he ignored the shadows, pounding down the boardwalk. Bryant called after him to stop. Ignoring the words, he listened to an inner urging. One that commanded him to head home.

"Protect her. Hide her under your feathers." Part of a verse from one of the Psalms came to him as he raced. Feathers, of all things to remember. No matter, he repeated the prayer over and over.

Feet sounded behind him and a hand grabbed his arm. "You can't go in there like a crazy man," Bryant hissed. "You don't even know if Blakenship's at your place."

The snap of a revolver cut through the sleepy quiet of Bailey's Meadow. The report sounded in front of them. In the dark, Onie turned to frown at the other man. "Convinced?"

"Yeah," the detective agreed. "Best head there quick."

The two took off again, only slowing as they rounded the corner and spied the back of the warehouse. A figure Onie recognized hurried to the door. As Bryant aimed his rifle, the sheriff put out a hand to lower the barrel.

"That's Harper. He watches the house at night." Onie growled darkly, "He'll have some explaining to do about how a man got past him."

A realization came to Onie when an eerie feeling raced through his whole body. Suddenly, it seemed this battle was as much a spiritual one as it was actual physical danger. Evidently, this danger created strange ideas for him. In that minute, he wondered if evil gave Blankenship the ability to be invisible.

To clear his head of such thoughts, he shook it. Next to him Bryant harrumphed. "No use waiting. Let's take a look through the windows."

A cloud moved, miraculously. The moon shone down on the warehouse, revealing one open window. A sure sign of where to go, unseen by them until the sudden light from above.

The men hunched as low as they could to sneak up to that window. A voice he did not recognize came to Onie's ears. It was a good sign they truly found Blakenship.

Of course, it also proved the blackguard was in there with Sookie and Wren. That wasn't good at all.

Another possible complication flitted into Onie's mind. It rang like a warning bell. Where was Harper? He saw the man enter the house.

A shrill screech rang out from the room. As if a spring sat under him, Onie popped up and aimed the Peacemaker into the room. With very little light, neither he nor Bryant could get a clear shot. The other man abandoned the window and ran for the door while Onie stayed where he was, waiting.

The scratch of a match preceded soft candlelight. Relief rushed through him when he saw his wife's face feathered by the flickering glow. While strain pinched her features, she appeared unharmed.

Feathers. Another fleece laid before the Lord to strengthen Onie's faith. Another odd thought while the wanted man might still be on the loose.

"My plan. This is *not* a part of my plan!"

Shrieks of rage came from the round man lying under Harper. The two wrestled for another minute or two. By the dim light, Onie saw hair gripped in Harper's hand. How had he ripped half of the other man's beard from his face?

He shook his head. Another strange thought. Pulling out a man's beard hair? He wondered if that was even possible. And yet, he saw it for himself.

In a low voice, he called to his wife. "Are you okay, sweetheart? Did he hurt you?"

The candle moved toward the men on the floor. It tilted and another light flared, revealing Wren's worried features. Rapidly, that first candle and his wife moved to the window.

She set the candle down and braced her hands on the window frame. Not signing anything, Sookie leaned out to him. At first, the touch of her mouth on his merely reassured. The kiss deepened with the force of relief and passion before she pulled away to beckon him inside.

"I'm coming. I want to hear how Harper ended up on top of our man there."

Responding, she chuckled. The hoarse, forced noise that formed her laugh reassured him as nothing else. She truly was safe.

Inside, he tucked his body out of the way as Harper and Bryant dragged a resisting prisoner past him. During it all, Blakenship continued to scream in a high, shrill voice for a key.

"I have to find it. I need it for my plan."

"I'm not giving you the key to these handcuffs." Bryant's voice mocked the other man. The prisoner ignored him and continued to wail.

Wren poked her head out of the bedroom to watch as Sookie passed her to head to Letty. The commotion woke the baby. Normally a sound sleeper, her daughter roared like a mountain lion when roused in the night. She stopped in mid-cry when her mother entered the room.

"Tell me what happened."

At Onie's command, Wren plopped onto the sofa. "What a night! That man grabbed me from my bed. With a gun, he forced me into your bedroom."

Onie had to ask it. "He didn't—"

"Thank God, no! I'm fine, only still jangled from being frightened." Wren threaded her hands through the hair on the back of her head and massaged the spot.

"I'm relieved. But please tell me the rest of what happened."

Onie sat in the chair opposite her and watched his sister-in-law by the kerosene lantern. "You must have seen how Harper got your attacker to the ground."

Screams started on the other side of the wall. Bryant and Blakenship were in the warehouse. The detective said he would send Harper to Ezra's house. That man could help them transfer Earl to a livery stall for the night and away from his captured boss.

Wren threw a worried glance at the wall. She turned to him and cringed at one particularly inhuman scream of rage. Relief filled her face as Sookie left the small bedroom and joined her on the sofa, wrapping her sister's hands in her own.

"I'm not sure." She pulled back to look at her sister. "Do you know how Harper got that man to the ground?"

Sookie held up her hand, palms in front of her chest and pushed. Onie's eyes widened. "He could get so close that he pushed him over?"

She nodded, and several curls hanging loose from her top knot danced on her shoulders and chest. It took effort to ignore his bride and finish the conversation. Nothing in his memory looked as precious as she did in that moment.

"Uh, Blakenship ranted while Harper simply sneaked up behind him?"

Again, a bob of her chin signaled agreement. At the movement, those beguiling curls danced, stirring his interest. He wanted to celebrate his wife's safety in a very private way. Mesmerized, he leaned closer to his sweetheart.

Sensing his interest, Sookie motioned with her palms up. Shaking them from side to side, she signed for him not to do something. He easily guessed what that something was even though Wren looked blankly between the two of them.

When Wren opened her mouth to ask, Sookie put up one palm facing outward to stop her question. She pointed ahead of her before tumbling her hands one over the other. Wren's face screwed up in a mutinous expression.

"In the future? I'm an adult. Tell me now." Her complaint held childish tones, contradicting her words.

Sookie ignored her and rose, motioning for them to follow her. Onie immediately understood. Very soon they would have guests. A few things needed talking out this night.

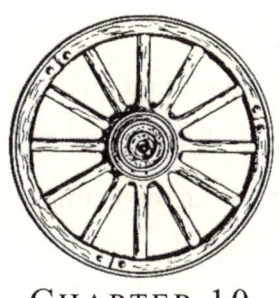

CHAPTER 10

"So, the key drove him crazy?" Wren sat at the table with Harper standing behind her. Bryant, Ruby and Sookie occupied the other three chairs while Onie and Ezra each stood at his wife's back.

Earl had to be removed from his cell. Bryant advised it. He wanted to keep the two from planning what to say so to escape the mess they'd created. Now, the shooter sat handcuffed to an iron circle inside one of Ezra's horse stalls. His bleated complaints sounded more like a sheep than a horse. At least, that's what Bryant told the criminal.

Behind the warehouse, people gathered in the kitchen and tried to ignore Blakenship's screams. The sound penetrated the wall which separated them from the main room of the warehouse. It grew softer after ten minutes or so. The man had to be growing hoarse.

"What will you do with him?" Wren translated her sister's gestures to the group.

Bryant's mouth rose on one side in a wry grin. "Let him escape. Maybe shoot him in the attempt?"

Fiercely, Sookie shook her head from side to side. Her sister reached across the table to squeeze her hand while Onie's hands hugged her shoulders. He leaned down to make shushing noises in her ear.

Wren's voice rang with a hard edge to it. "It's what he deserves. I'll never get over losing Father and Mother."

No one spoke. No one except Sookie. Her fingers flew as she *listened* to her sister. Wren nodded and let out a long, sad sigh.

"Yes, I can pray for the man's soul. Maybe facing his crimes will bring him to his knee. That man definitely needs the Lord." The young woman spoke by rote, as if she repeated something taught to her over and over.

Bryant pounded a fist on the table. "He'll face a judge for his crimes. I sent a wire to the nearest marshal. Maybe he'll bring a judge with him."

Harper took advantage of a lull in the conversation. "I understand his need for the key. What started him? Did he say why he targeted Mr. Donaldson and his family?"

This time Onie answered. "He keeps repeating about a plan. I can't get a reasonable word out of him otherwise. And I tried!" His voice ended on a disgusted note.

One more question from Harper had Sookie frowning. "Where is the key? What does it unlock?"

Sookie motioned and her sister rose. She left the room and returned only minutes later. The lovely blue enamel and gold of the locket pin glistened in the lantern light. She laid it in front of Sookie. Her sister once again tried to open the jammed catch of the locket.

A hand appeared, palm up, in front of her. "Please, let me. I know something about jewelry." Harper accepted the piece as she set it in his hand. With a small knife he fished from his pocket, the man carefully maneuvered it under the catch and between the two parts of the locket.

As the group watched, a slow smile caught fire and spread on the man's face when the locket sprang open. He set it down to let the others see the dull metal of a key. Around the table some frowned and others grinned in comprehension.

"For a lockbox, I think."

The other men nodded at Harper's suggestion. Sookie picked it up to rub the metal between her fingers. She gestured, and her sister moved to a cupboard. Wren pulled a small stack of paper and a pencil from it.

Taking them, Sookie rapidly scrawled across the paper. *The will? In the box?*

"We'll need you to come east and settle matters, Mrs. Hastings," Bryant said.

I have to teach.

Wren held her hand up to stop her sister's worries. "I will stay. Letty and I can move in with Ruby."

She looked to that kind woman who smiled her agreement. "That is, if my brother-in-law allows it."

Onie looked dubious. "How will you staying here help with the school?"

Wren threw him a look that said *I can't believe you don't get it.* "I'll start teaching the children so they will know Sookie's signs when she returns. I know her plans to introduce them while teaching nursery rhymes to the little ones."

She finished with a huff to her voice. "I *can* teach language and grammar to the older ones. That is, using the dictionary we created."

Ezra groaned. "Sounds like another town meeting."

Not long after, the group separated. Bryant went to the warehouse part of the structure to guard the prisoner. At last, Blakenship was quiet. Nonetheless, the detective warned them to expect more noise when the man saw him.

Harper accepted the offer of the parlor sofa for the night rather than sleeping in the trees. Ruby and Ezra gathered up their sleeping children from it so he could lay down. That little family happily headed home.

Much later in the quiet night, Onie clutched his wife to him. She satisfied him physically. Their coming together was unlike anything he experienced with other women. It went beyond bodies joining. In a strange way, he felt sad about that.

In his heart, he knew how badly he had abused this intimacy with other women. This was a sin he could only confess. There was no way to fix the past.

On some level, this God-sent woman completed him like no one else. Not even Alicia had shared this sort of bond with him. Sookie definitely was a gift from the Lord.

"I'll be miserable without you if you head to Massachusetts." He whispered the words and felt a drop of warm liquid hit his chest.

Reaching down, his finger traced her cheek and captured a tear with his fingertip. "Maybe your Mildred Crenshaw could take care of everything for you. It might be a wasted trip for you."

Her head shook against the arm tucked around her. He sighed. "I could go with you. Someone needs to be there to translate for you."

Her right hand rubbed down his forearm. While he savored the touch, Onie knew she was *speaking* to him and not caressing him. "*How*? Well, Josef

Schmidt will see to the freight. He already goes with me on every trip."

He mentioned that old man, Ezra's former father-in-law, and stroked his wife's arm absentmindedly. "Yes, that would be perfect. His wife will help keep the business's accounts up to date."

Sookie's arms circled his bare torso. She squeezed tightly, kissing his shoulder to let him know how happy the plan made her. She pulled back and put her hands together in the moonlight, flapping them like a bird.

He guessed what she meant. "What about Wren? I think she should stay with Ruby. It might be lonely here for her, and Ruby will watch out for her."

Sitting up, Sookie formed her arms into a cradle and rocked an imaginary baby. "*Letty*? Yes, we'll take her with us."

A strangled noise he guessed to be a sound of relief came from his wife's throat. He felt the same. They could be gone for weeks. Too long to be separated from their precious little girl.

The marshal never arrived. He sent a message telling them that trouble with rustlers detained him. Since they had the prisoner already, he wired them to take the man east. Back to the judge who issued the warrant.

Onie watched over Earl and Bryant focused on Blakenship as they traveled by train. The worried wife and mother held Letty close, silently sitting some distance away from her husband and the prisoners. With effort, she kept her eyes directed from them and wrestled with the need to forgive. She knew very well the deep hurt caused by hatred. It ate at a person's soul.

While Letty lay across her lap, napping through the long afternoons, Sookie muttered silent prayers. Her lips moved without sound, reminding her of the voice Blakenship stole from her. With each agony-filled prayer, the Lord brought blessing after blessing to her mind.

She lost her parents. She gained a husband and child. She lost her teaching job. A new school welcomed her. Through this abundance of quiet time, she learned something important. While the

Lord had not caused her troubles, he definitely guided her through them. All she needed was a willing heart and time spent with Him to start healing her grief.

By the time they arrived in Boston, Sookie and Letty longed to escape the train car. The little girl wanted to run and play. She'd been confined and shushed. Almost always an obedient child, Letty followed her mother's commands. By the end, even she grew rebellious and difficult.

Cousin Mildred stood on the station's platform with arms outstretched in welcome. Onie planned to join them later at Milly's home. He had a prisoner to deliver first.

Milly cooed over Letty. The girl enjoyed having a different lap to sit in and babbled to the older woman during their journey to the mansion. When they stopped in front of the large brick home, memories from her younger years came back.

Strangely, Sookie's memories of staying with this woman during a particularly wonderful trip to Boston filled her mind. Long ago, when she was six or seven and before Wren was born. At least, she guessed it to be around that time. Odd the memories hadn't come to her when she and her sister stayed here weeks before.

"By your face, I see that you remember being here. As a child I mean. You didn't recognize it on your earlier visit." Reaching around the baby in her lap, Milly patted the younger woman's hand. "Grieving as you were, I kept that memory to myself."

Sookie held her palms up skyward and raised her eyebrows. She tried to convey her one-word question. *Why?*

Milly looked at her. "I think you're wondering about something." She tapped her chin, thinking. "Perhaps you want to know why you didn't visit more often?"

Her cousin sighed deeply at Sookie's nod. "Your mother stopped traveling much after your sister's birth. She never recovered her energy from having babies so late in life."

It should hardly matter that she visited as a child, but Sookie felt a burning behind her eyes. The mother she missed felt closer than in months. From Milly's lap, Letty reached for her mother. Perhaps she sensed her sadness. In that moment, both past and future met as Sookie buried her face into her daughter's curly hair. She was taking her child to visit just as her mother had years before.

They spent a quiet evening. One small part of it stuck in Sookie's memory. An instance when she learned something she would always cherish.

Onie arrived by cab and used the mansion's door knocker. Hearing it echo through the lower part of the home, Sookie raced to the foyer. Seeing him in the doorway, her face and huge sigh started him laughing. While he crossed the foyer to her, she threw a "play" scowl his way.

Giving one final chuckle, he lifted her hands within his and pressed a soft kiss to each. "Why do you look relieved that I came? Didn't you know I'd move Heaven and Earth to get back to my bride?"

He mentioned her alone. He returned to her, not simply to Letty. To her. His bride.

Oh, but she did love this man.

Beside them, Milly released her own contented sigh. "I knew the Lord wanted me to send you to Nebraska, Sookie."

The woman pulled her lavender-scented square of linen from the reticule at her wrist. She dabbed a tear and beamed at them. "Such a happy thing to see you together."

After bathing to get rid of the grime and ashes from the train, that couple proved how right Milly was in matching them. Even in their most intimate times, they moved in tandem. Somehow, Onie sensed what thrilled her and taught her in turn.

As he lay on his back, sated, Sookie drew a heart on his chest with one finger. He grabbed it, laughing. "That tickles, woman. What are you doing anyhow?"

By the dim glow of the kerosene lantern, turned low to create coziness, Sookie sat up and put a fist to her heart. Then she pulled it away and pointed at her husband. At his silence, she repeated the motions. Each second stretched like hours while he looked at her without speaking.

Finally, he sat up and pulled her against him. "How can a woman as perfect as you love me?"

Sookie shook her head to deny his words. "Well, you're perfect to me. Perfect, even if my Sookie's silent."

Putting a hand behind her head, he lowered his mouth to hers. She expected a slow passionate kiss. This touch of lips spoke more of promise than passion. When he lifted his head, what she glimpsed in his face by the dim light confirmed that.

"Susan Kay Donaldson Hastings, I love you. Have loved you since that first smile from you at the train station." His laugh had a rich warm sound to it. "Felt like rockets exploding in my chest when I first saw your smile."

With her hair upswept and a new bonnet in place—a gift from her cousin that waited for her in the bedroom she'd used on her previous trip there—Sookie braved one more trip by train. The blue material that rippled in a pattern on the underside of its brim perfectly matched the traveling suit she wore. The dressmaker who made the suit, Cousin Mildred told her, provided the material for the bonnet.

Sookie dearly wanted to stay with her daughter and enjoy a quiet afternoon. Onie and Milly both determined that they should unlock the lockbox as soon as possible. Her cousin even wired a judge, a friend of her late husband, to meet them as a witness and act legal on whatever they found. The deceased Donaldsons' lawyer would also meet them at the bank.

An accommodating upstairs maid stayed with Letty. The little girl loved Milly's gardens and immediately liked Ellen, the maid. Still, Sookie left her daughter reluctantly as she left for the train station.

Familiar sights surrounded her as the three travelers arrived in Arnolds Corners. The forty-minute trip amazed Sookie. That wonderful day a month before when Milly rescued her and Wren, the trip seemed endless as Sookie sat by her sister. Dread filled her that day. Anticipation filled her today, a happy anticipation. She would see if her father provided for his daughters after all.

A bank clerk met them as soon as the trio entered the bank's lobby. He led them silently down a short hall and into a room where three men waited. Sookie recognized Robert Grant as well as Mr. Fellows, her father's lawyer. The only stranger in the room had to be Judge Patterson, she reasoned.

Introductions were made. During them, Sookie's gaze drifted often to the box on the table.

The locket pinned to her throat hung heavy with the important key hidden in it. Heavy with promise.

Judge Patterson's deep voice harrumphed before he rumbled out instructions. "Please, sit everyone. As befitting this type of situation, the deceased's lawyer will open the box and catalogue its contents. I stand ready to legally rule on any motions he puts to me."

Seated directly across from the attorney, Sookie moved her gloved hand under the table to rest on her husband's thigh. He understood immediately and took her trembling hand into his. Fingers caressed the palm through the black material, calming her. With her other hand, she gave the key to Mr. Fellows then pinned the locket again at her throat. Her hand sneaked under the table and back into her husband's loving grasp.

Stock certificates for Wells Fargo and the Union Pacific Railroad were among several in the box. Government bonds also went onto the lawyer's list of contents. A lovely set of pearls came next, bringing to Sookie's mind her eighteenth birthday when her parents gifted her with a similar strand. These had to be for Wren's upcoming birthday. That they bought them so far ahead prickled the flesh of her arms. Had one of her parents had a premonition of their death?

At the bottom, neatly folded in an envelope, her parents' will waited. Fellows read it aloud, his words turning Sookie and Wren into heiresses. Heiresses who spent six months in a filthy tenement because she couldn't open the heart.

The judge spoke words to probate her inheritance. Documents were signed. The judge transferred the house's deed into her name, a house in the well-to-do section of Arnolds Corners.

Sookie inherited everything, "With the understanding that she will care for her sister and provide her with an inheritance when she marries or reaches the age of twenty-one," her father had stipulated.

Surrounded by wise counsel, Sookie signed any questions she had and, thanks to her husband's help in translating, started in motion the sale of the business and house. Her former life, and Wren's as well, was gone. Nebraska was home now.

Fellows readily agreed with the sale. "You are in no position to run the business, but I will explore whether his partner intends to sell his half. I understand he needs money for an attorney." The attorney shook his head over that, having just learned from Onie about Blakenship's crimes.

"I already received two offers for the home. They came soon after your parents' deaths. Those buyers may have found other homes, but—" Fellows let the words hang in the air.

Sookie met his eyes and shrugged before tapping her finger to Onie's chest and then moving her hands in the sign for home. "My wife says that her home is with me. Sell it for a fair price to the next person who offers."

Not wanting to be away from Letty for too long, the couple nevertheless visited the family home. Amazingly her clothing and those of Wren hung in each sister's armoire. She instructed the housekeeper to see everything packed into trunks. If more trunks were needed, the woman would only need to send to The Emporium for them. The lawyer had instructions to settle any debt Sookie owed the store.

Hurriedly, the mute woman wrote out a list that included several items of furniture and dishes she wanted crated and shipped. Unhappily, she learned that Blakenship had already sold her mother's silver Sookie remembered from each of her mother's dinner parties.

Onie gave her a crooked grin at her sad look. "Don't worry. I expect a certain crime boss might get it back for us. I only need to put out the word and offer a reward as well as the cost of the sliver."

Paintings, her parents' portrait, and photographs. They all went on the list Sookie wrote out for the housekeeper. Watching at her elbow, Onie held up a hand. His stance bristled with agitation.

"We can't fit this lot into our few rooms."

Setting aside the steel pen, Sookie motioned with one fist atop the other in a repeated movement. Then she put two fingers together in what looked like a peaked roof. At the shake of Onie's head, her hands went to her hips.

"You want to build a house?"

A quick nod and smile answered him. Sookie rocked her arms as if they held a baby. She followed this by holding up three fingers.

"Three! You want at least three more children?" His agitation changed to a playful look that held a great deal of heat. "I expect I can help you with that."

EPILOGUE

Bailey's Meadow, Nebraska
Late October 1871

Wiley Schwartz turned away from the backdoor to
the house. Through the screen door, Sookie gave the
man's back only a cursory glance before focusing
on the telegram her husband held. When Letty tried
to escape the towel that held her to the kitchen
chair, her mother shooed her with fingers brushing
the air and returned to sit down to the interrupted
meal.

Onie also sat again at his spot at the short table's
head. They always ate a light lunch in the kitchen
and used the dining room only for dinner. She
refused to comply with the local custom of a heavy
dinner at noon and a light supper. Sookie brought

her eastern customs along with her furniture to Nebraska.

Wren was absent at lunch that day, being on a picnic with Reynolds Harper. The two had developed an easy friendship once Reynolds stopped what Wren called "his nonsense" about marriage. Maybe her sister's protest that she was a stranger to him slowed down his courting. Nowadays, the two enjoyed each other's company without his odd wooing.

While Onie opened and read it silently, Sookie's middle gave an odd clench. The baby inside was too small for her to already feel its movements. The strange sensation had to be a reaction to the telegram.

She stomped her foot once, bringing up her husband's head. He directed one arched eyebrow at her. "You don't want to know what's in this, do you?" He casually waved the telegram.

Playfully, she shook a fist at her husband. Letting the corners of her mouth turn sadly downward, she rubbed her stomach. He snorted and leaned back in his chair. From her spot, Letty imitated his snort and banged her spoon on the maple table.

"I know. Don't torment a woman who's expecting." He eyed her askance. "Seems to be you've used that one every day for the last three months since we knew about the baby."

Her lips wide in the smile that never failed to thrill Onie, Sookie playfully patted the small bulge of her belly. Onie's face lost its teasing expression. His eyes heated with a look that spoke to his wife about her pregnancy. Pride, contentment, and intimacy combined in the look to tell her how happy he was to have another child joining their family.

"Mama. Done." Eighteen-month-old Letty banged her spoon and grinned. Her six teeth gleamed white in her broad smile.

Her mama shook her head and pointed at the few carrots on the girl's small plate. Crossing her arms mutinously, Sookie's daughter scowled. "No eat." Even as she said the words, Letty shook her head as she signed *eat*.

Onie watched, astounded as always. The children at school were like Letty. They quickly grasped the signs and communicated easily with

Sookie. She taught three days each week, along with Wren, and the mayor realized after the first week what a treasure the town had in Onie's wife. He apologized soon after she started for demanding the trial period, too. Something that pleased Sookie since she had found his demand insulting.

He pushed thoughts of her classroom out of his mind and focused on the paper he held. Mildred sent it. As usual, it was long. The woman never bothered to worry over cost when she sent a wire.

Blakenship convicted. In Charlestown State Prison. Female dormitory. Woman in disguise. Took dead brother's identity. Will write more details in letter. Judge rescinded her ownership. Falsely bought share of Emporium. Business can now sell. Sending husband for Wren. Arriving two weeks with man.

Shaking her head vigorously, Sookie held up her hands palms out. Her husband swallowed his laugh and nodded gravely. "I'll wire her instructions to cancel any wedding plans for Wren. I'll tell her to come alone."

He looked down at the paper. "Why would the woman pretend to be a man?"

Sookie signed *power*. Her gesture for money came next. Her hands flew as he tried to follow the rapid speech.

Finally, he held up one hand. "Yes, I understand that Blakenship was fighting against a world controlled by men. But she murdered to get what she wanted. There is no excuse for that."

Sadly bobbing her head, Sookie's eyes showed the grief that still weighed heavily on her at moments like this. The spoon banged again, distracting her. Letty opened her mouth for her parents.

"Done," she insisted. The carrots disappeared. By the girl's sly look, Onie suspected they might be under her on the chair. Neither he nor Sookie had been watching like they usually did.

Using the towel that kept Letty in the chair, Sookie wiped the girl's face and hands. Then she snuggled her daughter close on her lap. Disgust twisted her mouth as she lifted her daughter and peeled smashed carrot from Letty's bottom. Grabbing the towel, Sookie wiped at the girl as well as her own pinafore that covered her light cotton, pink dress. Even in late October, Nebraska days could be hot. This year definitely proved that.

A snort drew her eyes. Onie's red face was nearly covered by his napkin. Behind it a sudden flood of laughter rang in the large kitchen of their newly built home. They'd only been in it one week and already it felt like home. Letty's giggles followed and Sookie joined in with her own tinkle of joyful laughter.

Yes, this was definitely her family. And this house was home.

Mildred Crenshaw is headed to Bailey's Meadow? Will she abide by Sookie's telegram and not bring a groom for Wren?

Has the matchmaker started sending mail-order grooms? That hardly fits with her goal to civilize the West one bride at a time. What is Milly's plan?

Find out the answers in *Wren's Wooer*, releasing November 2021.

Glossary

from Sookie's Dictionary

- Spin one finger in a circle pointing at the other person: AGAIN
- Hands up, palms out, and shaking them from side to side: STOP. THAT'S WRONG.
- Rubbing stomach: STOMACHACHE
- Lightly thump head: HEADACHE
- flap right hand out with the palm up: WHAT'S HAPPENING?
- Rubbing her right hand down her left forearm: HOW?
- Covering her eyes: DOESN'T WANT SOMETHING
- Spread hands apart with palms down: DONE
- Tapped chest at the same time as touching something: MINE

- lifted a finger and touched the invisible numbers on a make-believe clock: TIME
- opening her lips while she made a tumbling motion from them with one finger: ASK
- Crossing fingers: Sibling
- index fingers about two inches apart: SMALL
- turn in a circle with one of index finger pointing down: WORLD
- finger to her ear: HEAR
- stacked imaginary blocks one after another with her hands in front of her chest: VERY MUCH
- pursed lips: DON'T'S CODDLE ME.
- Hug her hands to her chest and shake back and forth: I'm so happy.
- Pointing over right shoulder: YESTERDAY
- Moving one fist atop the other in a repeated motion: BUILDING
- Fingers put together like a peaked roof: HOME

LEAVE A REVIEW

The End

If you enjoyed this story, I would appreciate it if you would leave a review, as it helps me reach new readers and continue to write stories that appeal to you.

Tap here to leave a review.

https://www.amazon.com/Marisa-Masterson/e/B07PRCNS49

Coming November 2021

Wren's Wooer

The third novel in the trilogy that started with *Ruby's Risk*!

BOOKS BY MARISA MASTERSON

Find these titles at
https://www.amazon.com//e/B07PRCNS49.

Most Popular!

kindleunlimited

Ruby's Risk

Westward Home and Hearts 2

A man might homestead, but it takes a woman to turn that place into a home!

The Proxy Brides

A Bride for Darrell (Book 17)

Can a man who never agreed to marry the proxy bride and a woman pursued by murderers make a life together?

A Bride for Bode (Book 21)

All thoughts of annulment disappear when Bode meets his proxy bride. The girl of his dreams! His violet who is neither shy nor wilting. So, will she remain married to him when she learns about his business?

A Bride for Bode (Book 49)

The surprise child given to her is not Frankie's, so why does she risk her marriage to keep the little girl? Frankie's worry is only about her proxy groom's reaction. She has no idea of the danger that follows the child—and now her also!

A Bride for Harland (Book 51)

Renie Hunter knows her proxy groom. At least she thought she did. The grumpy man who meets her train in New Mexico is more beast than handsome prince. Will she be able to reach his heart and rediscover tender man who wooed her years before?

Spinster Mail-Order Brides

A Farmer for Christmas (Book 4)

Will Myra's new husband let her give four motherless girls a happy Christmas?

A Shadowed Groom for Christmas (Book 6)

Married to a man in a mask, Kitty begins to wonder about her husband. Who or what lies under the hood he wears? Will she live to discover the answer?

A Keeper for Christmas (Book 12)

People say he crazy. His mail-order bride says the whole town must be blind! With danger stalking the couple, a Christmas miracle might be their only hope.

A Strongman for Christmas (Book 34)

Stranded at the circus, what will this mail-order bride do? Can she trust the strong giant who is built so much like her terrible brother? Wynona will need to decide quickly as danger has followed her from her hometown.

Ornamental Match Maker

MARISA MASTERSON

A Snowy Delivery for Christmas (Book 21)

Two lonely people in a cold rooming house. A good thing for them that their landlady has Christmas magic at her fingertips. Will strange twists and the abandoned baby lead to a Christmas wedding? Perhaps their landlady will need to step in with a miracle and a very special Christmas ornament?

Aloha My Love: Christmas in July *(Book 27)*

Two sneaky mothers and an appearance by Elvis add up to a Christmas in July that this couple won't forget in this quick, fun contemporary romance!

Belles of Wyoming

Grace for a Drifter *(Book 12)*

Will a grieving husband get the answers he needs to understand why he recognizes his dead bride leaving a hotel? faked her death? Amazingly, this couple is drawn into the mystery surrounding the disappearance of Grace's aunt. Will they work together or let old lies stand in their way?

The Teacher's Star *(Book 25)*

Rustlers and a mystified marshal. A treasure map and a missing child. Why does nothing make sense to this smart school teacher?

<u>Romance in Historical Wisconsin</u>

Hart's Longing

Sometimes a girl needs a hero to inspire her to action rather than merely being her rescuer.

Manny's Triumph

Will Carlene's determination and Manny's desire to save her be enough to give them a happy ending?

Wistful in Wisconsin

He was her rescuer. Would he also be the love of her life? Not if he has anything to say about it!

A Nurse for Niall

The surprise waiting for the young, crippled nurse will lead Alice into an unwanted marriage and a rivalry that threatens her only hope for a career and a home.

Adventurous Heroines

The Massachusetts Bride (North and South Book 7)

While the North and the South war, the battle of a married strangers stuck in an old farm house involves unfulfilled love and the tormenting nightmares. But what can a man do when his beloved wife prefers the cow's company?

Ginger Snap *(Lockets and Lace Book 25)*

True love picked a terrible time to grab Ginger Snap's heart. She saw the man she would love forever. He saw only a scruffy boy.

Detective to the Rescue *(Christmas Rescue Book 18)*

Her first case was a disaster! Pinkerton Agent Charity Melrose has one more chance to prove her worth and the life of a woman to save. With few clues to the victim's whereabouts, this could be her last case. And what to do with her fake husband?

ABOUT MARISA

Marisa Masterson and her husband of thirty-two years reside in Saginaw, Michigan. They have two grown children, one son-in-law, a precious granddaughter who visits daily.

She is a retired high school English teacher and oversaw a high school writing center in partnership with the local university. In addition, she is a National Writing Project fellow and a regular contributor to the Sweet Americana Sweethearts and Sweethearts of the West blogs.

Focusing on her home state of Wisconsin, she writes sweet historical romance. Growing up, she loved hearing stories about her family pioneering in that state. Those stories, in part, are what inspired her to begin writing.

Please visit Marisa's website at www.marisamasterson.com or spend time with her and other authors at https://www.facebook.com/groups/sweetwwreads.

If you like this book, please take a few minutes to leave a review now! Marisa appreciates it and you may help a reader find their next favorite book!

Made in the USA
Monee, IL
08 August 2021

74538746R00125